HIS TO TAKE

THE ROWDY JOHNSON BROTHERS
BOOK 1

TORY BAKER

Copyright © 2024 by Tory Baker

All rights reserved. No part of this book may be reproduced in any form or by any electronic or mechanical means, including information storage and retrieval systems, without written permission from the author, except for the use of brief quotations in a book review. No part of this book may be used to create, feed, or refine artificial intelligence models for any purpose without written permission from the author.

Please respect the author and do not participate in or encourage piracy of copyrighted materials that would violate the author's rights.

This is a work of fiction. Names, characters, businesses, places, events, locales, and incidents are either the products of the author's imagination or used in a fictitious manner. Any resemblance to actual persons, living or dead, or actual events is purely coincidental.

Cover Design: LJ with Mayhem Cover Creations

Editor: Julia Goda with Diamond in the Rough Editing

Proofreader: Rosa with Fairy Proofmother Proofreading

Photographer: Katie with Cadwallader Photography

Models:

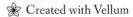 Created with Vellum

*"Don't be afraid to go after what you want to do,
and what you want to be.
But don't be afraid to be willing to pay the price."
- Lane Frost*

Playlist

THE ROWDY JOHNSON BROTHERS

Tory Baker on Spotify

BLURB

I'm a man who knows what he wants and what I want is Birdie.

It hurt like hell to watch her leave our small town to set off and chase her college dreams. I let her go once, I'm not letting it happen again.

Now she's home for good, and I'll stop at nothing to keep her with me, *always*. Even if that means tying her to me in every way possible.

Are you ready for the first book in the Rowdy Johnson Brothers? This cowboy may be the youngest of six but he's not afraid to go after what he wants, on the ranch, in the saddle, and the woman he loves.

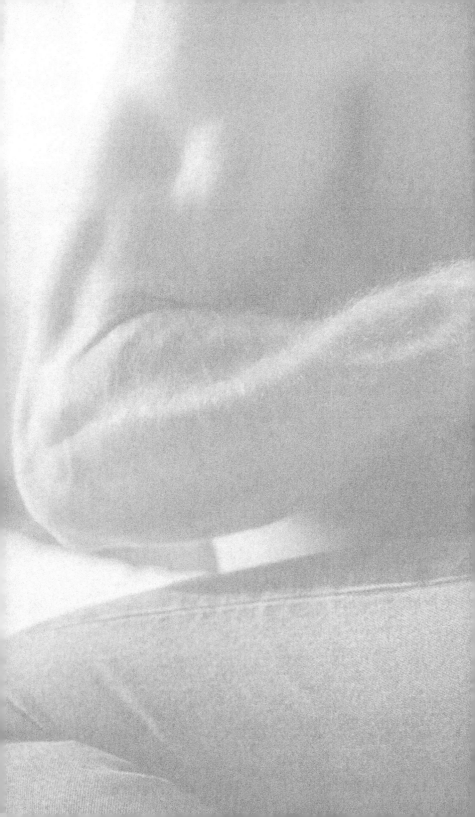

PROLOGUE
LANE

Four years and a few months earlier

"LANE." I look up from where I'm working, already knowing the owner of that voice. Beatrice "Birdie" Robertson is making her way toward me, and the fence I was working on can now wait. She's more than worthy of all my attention. I watch as she walks toward me while I stand up from my crouched state, taking off my hat to wipe away the sweat with my forearm before putting it back in place.

There's no denying the attraction I feel for Birdie, from my heart to my damn dick. They both perk right up whenever she's near. Hell, even if she isn't around. The slightest hint of Birdie, and I'm ready to abandon whatever the fuck I'm doing and go after her. My eyes soak in her beauty, from her boot-covered feet to her bare shoulders. She's in her normal attire for summer —a tank top of some type and cutoff jean shorts.

There's a tight smile on her face, no longer relaxed like I left her in my bed this morning. That was after I woke her up with my cock sliding in and out of her tight heat. Leaving her naked and in my bed was hard as hell, especially in her fuck-drunk state and slowly falling back asleep, but I had shit to do, and if I'd stayed any longer, my brothers would give me a ration of shit.

"Babe," I reply. I've heard her say my name in many ways—when she's happy, when she's worried, when she's sad, and when she's breathless. The last one being my favorite. Right now, there's a difference in her tone. The outside world may think it's full of joy. It's not. Sure, she's putting on a brave face and trying to hide the strain in her voice, and there's no way I'm going to let something bring her down when I can fix it.

"Lane," she repeats my name. She's closer now, and I can see the tightness around her eyes and lips. Gone is the soft and pliant woman from this morning. My gut sinks as I think the worst. Birdie and her mom live on the neighboring ranch, one of the three, along with ours. Each corner butts up to one another. They only moved here to Arrowleaf, Wyoming, last year. Birdie's mom bought old man Keller's ranch when he was ready to retire. His kids didn't want to take over the family farm, and as much as my family wouldn't have minded adding to our own ranch, we had plenty of land and work. Mom and Dad are still very hands-on, as are my five older brothers. Now Ms. Robertson, Birdie's mom, turned the old cattle ranch into a flower farm, and from what I can see and hear, it's doing damn good.

"Baby, everything okay?" She shakes her head yet smiles, giving me not a fucking hint of what could be bothering her.

"Yes, no, maybe." My hands move to her waist, pulling her closer as soon as she's within reaching distance. Birdie's hands rest on my shoulders, not caring a bit that I'm a sweaty mess. I dip my head. One thing for sure, I need a taste of her on my lips, and she needs to know I'm here, no matter fucking what. Her eyes close, a sigh escapes, and my tongue licks at her lower lip until she opens for me. I use my teeth to nip where I just licked, knowing exactly what she wants and needs. Only then do I allow our tongues to meet. She melts into my body, fingers gripping my slick skin beneath my shirt, and as much as it pains me to pull away, if I don't, we'll be doing a hell of a lot more than talking.

"Better?" I ask once our kiss ends.

"A little." Her hazel eyes meet mine for a moment before she looks over my shoulder. Clearly, things are not alright, and it's going to be me who pries it out of her.

"Birdie, you can tell me anything."

"I know. This is just hard. I don't want to have to pick between you and college, but there's no other option, Lane. It's stay here and go to the local college or take the full-ride scholarship in Colorado." Well, fuck, no wonder she's a mess of emotions.

"That's fucking amazing. I'm so damn proud of you." All Birdie has ever wanted to do is go to college, be the first one in her family to have a degree and walk across the stage with her diploma.

"Yeah, but that means I have to choose between you here or college in Colorado." I'll be damned if I make her choose between me or her dream. This sucks, big time, but what kind of man would I be if I asked her to stay?

"Don't choose me. I'm not going anywhere. When you come home, this is where I'll be, okay?" I can see the turmoil in her eyes, the way she's trying to breathe through the pain and attempting to keep it together.

"Lane, I can't ask for you to wait for me." Her voice is muffled since her face is planted in my chest. My hands move to her lower back, sliding beneath the cotton fabric of her tank.

"And I can't ask you to do the same thing either." My hands travel up the sides of her spine, feeling the lack of clothing beneath the fabric. Goddamn, my cock should not be making its presence known at this time. I lost her hands on my shoulders when she decided to burrow into my chest. Now, her thumbs are hooked in the belt loops of my jeans, and the rest of her fingers are sliding up and down my lower abdomen.

"Make it go away. Make the pain go away. Please, Lane." This won't help her, not in the long run. It's still gonna hurt like hell, but if this is the comfort she needs, well, I'm going to be the selfish ass and take what she's giving to me so freely.

"You sure this is what you want?" Birdie's head is tipped up, the redness in her eyes giving her away, yet she is holding it together.

"I'm sure." I pull her shirt up, she lifts her arms, and I'm greeted with the sight of her bare tits, hard nipples, and pebbled flesh.

"That's all I need to know." I drop the shirt to the ground. She kicks off her boots, one after the other, and our hands work simultaneously on the button of my jeans. It's not until I feel her hand wrap around my cock, slowly sliding up and down, moving at a slow and steady pace, that I know she's not going to stop unless I make her. I move faster to remove my boots. There's no fucking way she's going to try and get me off when she hasn't come at least twice.

"Lane, God. I need you." I bend at the waist enough to grasp the back of her thighs, lift her off the ground, and carry her to the bed of my truck.

"You're getting me, Birdie, all of me." The tailgate is down, the back of her thighs meets the warm metal, and my hands work on her jean shorts as my mouth wraps around one of her berry-tipped nipples.

"Lane." She arches her body up, begging for more. My hand skims down her abdomen, the tips of my fingers feeling her quiver. I suck harder, deeper, pulling on her nipple. My hand slides lower, cupping her smooth bare pussy, one finger dipping farther, feeling her wetness coating me. Goddamn, this woman is everything, and if this is my last taste of Birdie Robertson, I'm going to make it last. All fucking day.

1

LANE

Present Day

"HAPPY BIRTHDAY!" I walk inside my parents' house, unprepared for the celebration they've somehow managed to put together. After the day I've had, all I want is to go home, take a hot-as-fuck shower, drink a beer, and sleep the rest of the day away.

We've been moving cattle all week, rotating them to a different pasture. Of course, problems came along with it—more downed fencing, rotted poles, and then one of the guys who we just hired had an accident. None of us could predict that on his first day, Dale would slice the length of his forearm wide open. The fabric of his shirt did nothing to protect him when he let go of the barbwire too soon. After the nurse we have on the ranch took one look at his wound, she loaded him up in her car to head to the hospital. Dale ended up with thirty stitches and is out for the next week or so. This means we'll be pulling double duty to get shit together, given we're down a man. Happy fucking birthday to me.

"Thank you." I plaster a smile on my face, one I'm sure is fake as fuck. This is as good as it's gonna get. Honestly, if it weren't for my dad laying it on thick about Mom making my favorite meal and dessert, I wouldn't be here at all. So thick, he let me know exactly what she was making: jalapeño poppers with a few other appetizers, prime rib, twice-baked potatoes, and whatever vegetable she had on hand. As long as the vegetable Mom makes is smothered in garlic and butter, I'll eat it. Then he followed up the schmoozing with another, adding brownies and vanilla ice cream to the mix. Mom knows I'm not a fan of cake or cupcakes. They're too damn sweet, and the icing makes it ten times worse.

"My baby, happy birthday, sweetheart," Mom whispers into my ear. She's the first one to come up and give me the greeting without the whole group. My eyes take in the room. Our family is here, and so are a few other families from the surrounding ranches. Eleanor, Birdie's mom, nods her head my way, and I return the sentiment. Every year, I tell them I don't want or need anything big. A small dinner, which is hard considering between my parents and brothers, there're eight of us, which is more than enough.

Tonight is a bit different. There are more people here than usual, and I'm trying to figure out why the hell they'd think I'd want something like this after working all day.

"Thanks, Mom," I reply, pulling away. She holds my shoulders, and I'm not going anywhere until she's done saying whatever she has to say.

"You're welcome. I know, I know. This isn't your idea of fun, but humor me, will you? Also, Birdie's home." That was not what I expected to hear coming from my mom. The wind is knocked out of my sails. The last I heard, she was staying in Colorado indefinitely. Birdie only came home on rare occasions, like holidays and her mom's birthday. I made sure anytime she was here, I wasn't. I took the work my brothers passed up. Hauling cattle, dealing with grunt work, it didn't matter. As long as I wasn't home, all the better.

The need to try and change her mind to stay home was all I wanted. That wouldn't be fair to her. She would have stayed, then she'd have grown to resent me, and no fucking way did I want that for either of us. The day she left to head to Colorado, I knew it was time to let her go. My gut was in knots and my heart, well, I'm not going to talk about that worthless organ when it comes to Birdie.

"She here?" I ask, my eyes glancing around the crowded house. A lot of the older houses around here don't have an open floor plan. Mom and Dad changed that in the last five years.

Birdie isn't in sight. My brothers are, though. They're crowded around the kitchen island, no doubt getting their grubby hands on the appetizers. By the time I get a chance for some, I'm sure they'll be gone. Fucking brothers, man. You can't live with them, and you damn sure can't live without them.

Dad is in the corner, talking to another neighbor. They're no doubt discussing the next hay season and what's going to happen in town with the new mayor taking over. Basically, when Dad and Mike get together, it's a bitch fest, and I'd much rather deal with what Mom is throwing my way.

"No, Ellie tried to get her to come, but she wasn't having it. The drive was terrible with traffic or some such thing." Mom shrugs her shoulders, trying to make light of the situation, but that doesn't stop the knot in my gut from tightening further.

"Alright, I'm going to go make my rounds." The angel on my right shoulder is telling me to stay put. *Your mom and family did this for you. The least you can do is say hello to everyone and stay through dinner.* The devil on my left shoulder is saying *Fuck it, turn on your booted fucking heel and go after the woman you let go.*

"Lane." Mom starts to say something but thinks better of it, going as far as to shake her head.

"Mom?" I question. We've gone through this

plenty of times. She didn't raise six boys without a mother's intuition for nothing.

"There's plenty of time for you to walk over to Birdie's, you know." A smile crosses her face, and the angel on my shoulder is gone now. There's no way I'm not going to take this opportunity and go after the woman I know down to the marrow of my bones is mine.

"Thanks, it shouldn't take long." I bend down, kissing her cheek, and say, "Try to keep your troublemakers from eating all of my birthday dinner, will you?"

"I can't make any promises, which is why you should get out of here." I take another sweep of the room on the off chance Birdie has made a sudden appearance. She hasn't, and that's my sign to head out the door before the rest of the crew descends. I've got a woman to go after.

2

BIRDIE

"I SHOULD HAVE BROUGHT Rocky and Tully home with me." I move to the bay window, looking out at the open expanse of Mom's farm. The beauty is growing more so as the sun slowly sets over the expanse of flowers.

When I pulled off the main road and onto Mom's dirty driveway, I was greeted with buttercups, Indian paintbrushes, goldenrods, and sunflowers. The variety of flowers was vibrant in color, and it calmed my nerves for the first time since things went to hell in Colorado. Not to mention seeing Mom waiting for me, standing on the front porch, hands together, attempting to stop herself from running down the steps before my car was parked.

She couldn't hold back after I was out of the car. I braced for impact, thinking it would help.

You know, holding your breath while pain is radiating from the inside out with only a hug. A hug you should be able to enjoy, yet I couldn't, and I couldn't tell her the truth either. Not in that moment, maybe not ever.

When she asked about my best friend, Tully, and my dog, Rocky, a mini Australian shepherd, I had to think quick on my feet. Tallulah changed her entire game plan. No, I take that back. *We* changed our plans entirely. Tully was going to head back to her family's place to work in the family business at the veterinarian's office her parents and brother owned. I was supposed to stay in Colorado in the small condo I was going to rent on my own. You know, trying to make things work with someone who isn't Lane Johnson and go on with life.

What a big fat waste of time and energy.

Luckily for me and Tully, her family was okay with her coming to Wyoming with me, probably because she focused her studies on livestock and large animals in the veterinary field, whereas her family is more in the companion specialty. They have a great family circle, a lot like Mom and I do. Especially since it's been the two of us for over fifteen years now.

Dad took off one day and never came back. We stayed in the same house for a year while Mom busted her ass to maintain a too-big house until she finally said enough was enough. We moved into a smaller house with less to maintain and stayed there until high school. All the scrimping and saving paid off. Mom made her dream come true and has absolutely done amazing. Her flower fields are used for arrangements all around the state, and once the wedding and holiday seasons calm down, she even opens the fields to the public.

You're such an idiot, Birdie. This is where you belonged all along. To be fair, the only good things that came from going away to college were my degree, my best friend, and my dog. Tully was the first person I called. She came to my rescue and has continued on her mission all along. Operation *Get Birdie out of Colorado* as fast as possible was in full effect.

Tully is also the only one who knows my truth. Okay, fine, it's a secret. A big fat embarrassing secret, one I made her pinkie swear not to tell a soul until I was ready. She's now bringing her things, my things, and Rocky. I'd have taken him with me, except he was at doggy day care, and it was an extra stop. Tallulah promised she'd pick him up the second I left town, and she did, too. Even went as far as FaceTiming me the second he was back with her. When I say Tully is a godsend, she truly is.

She loaded my car and stayed on the phone with me for the majority of the six hours it took me to drive home, and I'm not sure I'll ever be able to repay her. The drive went by fast. People have no idea how we can talk as much as we do, but we are the type of best friends who never run out of things to say.

Mom helped off-load the couple of bags I did pack. A miracle when she grabbed the one off the floorboard because carrying anything right about now would have hurt even worse. All that was left was the rolling suitcase. I took it by the handle, being sure not to tug it too hard. The last thing I wanted to do was jar myself and let out a loud cry.

I've made so many mistakes, and my heart drops to my feet every time I think about the pain I've caused along the way. They're tremendous, like leaving Arrowleaf, leaving Mom, and, of course, leaving Lane. I almost begged him to make it work long distance, then thought better of it. How wrong it would've been for me to ask him to wait.

That's why when Mom suggested I go to Lane's birthday party tonight, I balked. She let it slide. Whether she knew the reasoning or not, Mom didn't say. If I saw Lane right now, I'd break down, and my carefully built wall would crumble. I stayed back, took a hot shower, a short nap, and hid in my room until I heard the back screen door close.

This is why when I hear the same door Mom used nearly twenty minutes ago open, I spin around. My body protests the entire time, but it's also when my world spins on its axis. Standing in the doorway is Lane Johnson and his eyes are locked on me.

3

LANE

IT'S BEEN TOO FUCKING long since I've set my eyes on Birdie, and even though I'm fifteen feet away from her, all I can see is her.

Her pretty hazel eyes.

Her long brown hair.

Her soft, pillowy lips.

And her curves. Damn, she's only gotten curvier.

"Lane." Her voice is low and raspy. I bet she has no idea what it does to me when she says my name.

"Birdie," I reply as I step inside, holding the wood screen door behind me so it doesn't slam on my booted heels. I'd have thought she'd start walking toward me, but it seems that's not the case. She isn't meeting me halfway, not even when I've almost reached her. Birdie is rooted in place, back to the window, the setting sun glowing around her body. What I'm shocked to see the most is what she's wearing. A threadbare shirt, one of the many she swiped from me. This one is white, a horse on its hind legs, a man with a lasso, and our town name with the rodeo emblazoned beneath.

"It's your birthday. You should be with your family."

"No, here with you is where I should be. Word on the street is you're back for good. That true?" Birdie nods, her teeth pressing into her plush bottom lip, and damn if I can hold back. If anyone is going to bite her lips, it's going to be me. I take another step closer, hands cupping her cheeks, and when she doesn't pull away, I know I've got her right where I want her.

"Yeah, I'm home. For good." My head dips, my lips capture hers, and while my hands are holding her where I want her, Birdie's move to my chest, not pushing me away but pulling me closer. Her small fingers dig into my shirt and muscles, making my body want a fuck of a lot more. For right now, I'm going to settle on her lips. When she lets out that little purr in the back of her throat, I'm going for more.

Birdie may be older. May have been gone a long-ass time, but a lot remains the same. She tastes sweet, like berries, but with a hint of darkness. I pull her lower lip into my mouth, sucking on it as she moves her hands lower in a kneading movement. I'm not even sure she knows the noises she makes when I'm around, usually when we're kissing or she's asleep, like a kitten with their pawing behavior when they're nice and relaxed. Birdie gives me the sign she wants more. That purr I was after comes, allowing me to slide my tongue inside her mouth. And I take more while she gives it to me so freely. Her tongue chases mine while my hand that's holding her cheek slides to the back of her head and her long, dark hair tangles with my fingers.

"Lane," she breathes when I pull back for a moment, wanting to see the desire written all over her face. Damn, she's perfect—eyes hooded with lust, cheeks flush—and this time, when I seal my mouth to hers, I don't hold back. Years of pent-up frustration, with myself, with Birdie, with the whole fucking situation. I tried to come off like shit would be okay, but deep down, I was a damn miserable fool. While I continue our kiss, my hand is itching to see what she has beneath her shirt. The last time we were together, I'd get out of bed before her, do the morning chores, come back, make a cup of coffee, and sit on the back porch looking over the endless beauty of the family ranch. Birdie would meander her way out, a cup of coffee in hand, one of my shirts on her body, and stand next to me. The minute she'd finally wake out of her sleeplike stupor, she'd give me her lips. I'd slide my hand up the back of her leg and feel nothing but smooth, bare skin.

"Lane, please, more." I pull back, my hand

meeting the cheek of her ass and holding it there even though the tips of my fingers are begging to dip closer, ready to feel her wet center.

"You sure?" I ask.

"Yes, God, yes." She takes a slow and steady breath, her watchful eyes on me as I drop to my knees. My hands glide to the outside of her thighs. The only thing she's wearing is her shirt. It does nothing in the way of hindering my breathing in her scent. Christ, I've missed everything about Birdie, especially this.

"Going to make this last, Birdie. I hope you're prepared to hold on and enjoy the ride," I mutter, my head dipping beneath her oversized shirt, not bothering to pull the fabric up. I've got one task, and that's reminding her what it means to be mine.

Fucking heaven, that's the only way to describe what I'm feeling right now. Wetness is glistening along her slit, and my hunger for her takes over. My tongue glides along the outer edges, not moving directly to the source at first. We're both going to enjoy this and as her flavor explodes on my tongue, a groan leaves my body. My hands tighten on the cheeks of her ass, fingers dipping deeper, pulling her open, and she gets the message. She widens her stance, giving me more room to work with. There's no more holding back. I can't, not with the soft little sighs and moans leaving her with each swipe of my tongue.

"Lane." The tips of my fingers move closer, one pressing on an entirely different entrance. Birdie was hesitant when we first explored her ass years ago, my tongue rasping along her tightness, my finger pushing inside, and when she was ready, she took my cock as she fucked her pussy with a vibrator.

"You want that, baby? You want my fingers in your ass while I fuck your pussy with my mouth?" My words are muffled against her core. I can feel the tremble in her body. It's all the answer I need. My tongue invades her center, my finger pressing on her entrance, feeling the tight ring of her ass taking me so good. Her legs quiver. My hands are the only reason she's able to remain standing. I soak in her pleasure. It gives me pleasure of my own in return. I push in and out of her ass, my tongue doing similar to her cunt while my teeth rasp along her clit. It's the perfect trifecta as she falls apart for me, completely and totally unaware of how my cock is begging to do the same exact thing.

"Lane." My name escapes in a breathless plea. Whether it's for me to stop or to keep going, I'm not sure. One thing I do know is that leaving her after delivering the first of many orgasms is pure fucking torture. I place another open-mouthed kiss on her clit, reluctantly pulling my fingers away from her ass and back away. I'm on my feet. This time, I'm taking her shirt off. I want to see Birdie in nothing but bare skin.

"Gonna take you now, Birdie. Going to feel you like I did with my mouth, but this time, it's going to be my cock." My hands grip the edges of the fabric and pull it up, seeing more of her than when I was on my knees.

I look into her eyes. She's back to biting her bottom lip again. My eyes don't know where to look at first. It's when my eyes return to her body I see what has her all of a sudden locked up tight. Her arms aren't lifting up to help me take her clothes off. Instead, they're staying put by her sides, and it's only when I pull the shirt up to her abdomen that I know the reason.

"What the fuck, Birdie? What the hell happened?" I inch closer, abandoning her shirt. Crowding her while cupping her face once again. A burning in my gut rolls through my whole body. Someone hurt my woman so badly there's a print of a shoe. Her whole stomach is covered in blue and purple marks.

"I'm okay, Lane. I mean, I've got some healing to do, but it looks a lot worse than it is." She's being entirely too unconcerned about this, and there's no damn way I'm letting the subject lie. My body is rock fucking solid, yet my cock isn't hard any longer. The surge of anger is so bad that I'm sure steam is rising from my ears. All I can imagine is Birdie being hurt and alone with no one there to help her, left lifeless. Son of a bitch. This could have been so much worse. I know she's lucky, but that doesn't mean I have to fucking like it, or I'm not going to shoulder some of the blame.

I lift an eyebrow, my jaw clenched, and if my hands weren't on hers, my fists would be much the same way. "I'm okay. I'm better than it may seem. It looks worse than it is. I know you're going to want the whole story. Maybe we could move to the couch? I'm kind of feeling light-headed after, you know." Her cheeks have a tinge of color. She's still the same woman, only a few years older.

"Yeah." I take a step back. "Fuck, I don't know where to touch you now, baby." I'd pick her up and carry her to the couch, except that would probably hinder her more than help her.

"Lane, if you don't touch me, I'm going to hurt you worse than I already am." Her hand covers mine, taking it off her cheek, albeit she's moving gingerly as she does.

"Message received loud and clear." My words are gruff, and thankfully, she knows my fury isn't geared toward her. I'd cut my damn heart out for Birdie before I'd ever think of hurting her.

4

BIRDIE

I WRING my hands together as I sit down on my mom's floral couch. It's the same one she's had since we moved to the farm all those years ago. Us Robertson women are built differently. We didn't come from a background where spending frivolously was a luxury. We watched our pennies, lived within our means, and only bought what we needed.

While my childhood wasn't always the easiest on Mom, she made it work. I never knew she was struggling. She made it look like we were living the good life. There was no starving, no me coming home without her home, my clothes were nice even if they were thrifted. She made it work —dance parties in the kitchen, picnics in the living room on Friday nights along with a movie, and on the rare occurrences she had to work on the weekends, well, she'd take me with her, then we'd do something fun afterward.

"Lane, sit next to me, please?" He's treating me like I'm made of glass, which I understand. The bruising is bad, and while I'd like to say it doesn't hurt, that would be a bald-faced lie. The drive from Colorado to Arrowleaf was not easy, especially with the traffic in the city. Then, I obviously had to hide everything from Mom, another task that had me on edge, attempting to ebb some of the pain without holding myself.

"Birdie, baby. I'll sit in the chair. I don't want to jostle you any more than I already have." I'd laugh if it didn't hurt.

"Shut up and come sit next to me. I'm fine. Today is better than yesterday." I grab the pillow, place it across my chest, and hold it to my body. Tully told me the best thing to do is to keep my ribs unwrapped, take as many deep breaths as possible, and not stay in one position too long. Well, that was easier said than done with the six-hour drive that took closer to seven. "What I'm going to tell you has to stay between us. There's an open investigation, and I was told the less others know, the better for the time being."

"I'm not liking this, Birdie, not at fucking all." Lane finally sits down and runs his fingers through his hair while breathing out what seems like the longest breath possible. I know what he's doing. Lane Johnson is struggling to get himself under control.

"I'm okay." I pause, trying to figure out where to begin that won't have him ready to go back to his house, grab his baseball bat or shotgun, and go after my boss and his son.

"Not buying it, Birdie, not in the fucking least." He looks at me, really looks at me. His blue eyes are the shade of the sky without a cloud in sight. They can change from light to dark depending on his moods and also what he's wearing.

"Well, I guess you're not wrong there, but I will be okay. I'm home, even though I didn't think it would take being beaten to bring me home." I press the pillow tighter, trying to block the emotions out, and Lane, the patient man he is, waits until I'm ready to continue.

"I was leaving Sherman Digital when it all went down. The owner's son asked if I wanted to grab a cup of coffee. I already had plans. Rocky was waiting for me at doggy day care. So, I told him no, but he proceeded to ask me out again, this time for drinks. I politely declined.

"Like I said, Rocky needed to be picked up, and my creep radar was already going off. So I slowly walked toward my car. He followed me the entire time. Apparently, Sherman Jr. doesn't know what no means. Once I made it to my car, things went from bad to worse.

"My keys weren't in my hand like they usually are, and he grabbed me when I was digging through my purse for them. I didn't see him coming. My fight-or-flight instinct did nothing for me. When he grabbed me, I was in complete shock."

I blink back tears, remembering the way he grabbed my upper arm, spinning me around because I went silent on him. I figured remaining quiet would be better than to poke the bear.

"You don't have to tell me if it's too hard for you, Birdie." Lane slides closer, his hand covering mine on my lap. He threads our fingers together and holds mine in his.

"It's alright. My keys ended up being my saving grace once I finally wrapped my hands around them inside my bag. Of course I lost my footing, ending up on the ground. And it was either protect my body while he was in a fit of rage or use the pepper spray on my key ring." That's when Sherman Jr. went after me, kicking me in my stomach before using his foot to step on me at the same time I sprayed him in the face." I take a deep breath or as much as I can with the bruising and continue with my story wanting to get it over and done with.

"Once he was busy crying about his eyes, I got up as fast as I could and locked myself in my car. My tires burned rubber with how fast I left the parking lot. I couldn't go get Rocky. The only place I could go was back to my apartment shared with Tully. She's a vet and was already home. This happened yesterday. Tully doctored me up, called the doggy day care, and asked for them to keep Rocky overnight.

"In the meantime, she took pictures, documented everything, and we called the cops. A lot is still left up in the air. I called Mom and told her there was a change of plans and I was coming. She welcomed me, Tully, and Rocky. They should be here in the next few days.

"So, yes, I had planned on staying in Colorado long enough to get my feet wet, but I knew I'd come home. I just didn't know it would be under these circumstances."

I stop talking. My ribs are starting to hurt, as well as the rest of my body. A lot has happened in the last twenty-four hours, and while, yes, Tully watched over me last night, I still didn't sleep very much. Truth be told, I probably won't until she and Rocky are out of that shithole.

"You left a lot out, but I get it. It's a lot to process and deal with, but later on, you'll tell me more when you're ready." Lane brings my hand to his mouth, kissing my knuckles before standing up. "Right now, you need to get horizontal, close your eyes, and sleep."

"And I can do that on my own. Today is your day. Don't make me feel bad for ruining the party happening at your parents'." With my hand still in Lane's, he helps me up from my seat.

"I've already got what I want for my birthday." My eyes close. This is the Lane Johnson I never should have left, the selfless, fierce protector and all-around amazing man.

"Lane."

"You rest. We'll work out the rest later." I nod. There's not a chance in hell I have the strength to argue with this man. Lane leads me toward my room one slow step at a time. When Mom walked me into my childhood room earlier, I realized she had never changed a thing. It seems like Lane will be seeing it as well.

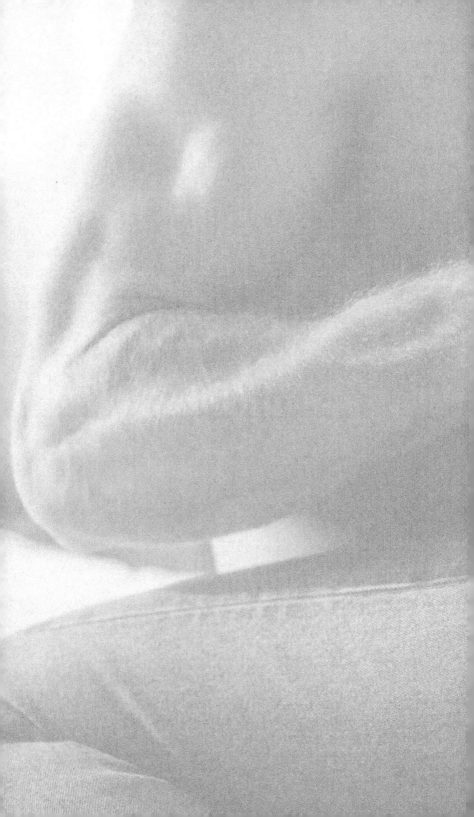

5

LANE

"I'LL BE JUST A MINUTE," Birdie tells me, making a detour to the hall bathroom.

"You need help, holler. Now isn't the time to hurt yourself worse." I'm sure I already made her pain ten times worse already. Greedy, that's what I am when it comes to Beatrice "Birdie" Robertson. Any place, anywhere, and any damn time I'm around her.

"I hear you." She doesn't look back as she walks her sultry self into the bathroom and closes the door behind her. I've been inside her pussy, her ass, her mouth, and taken numerous showers with her. Yet, going to the bathroom, she closes the door. Some things never change. Since I'm not heading back to Mom and Dad's anytime soon, I pull my phone out of my back pocket. I'll bet Birdie hasn't eaten yet either. Maybe her mom will bring us both a plate or at least maybe mine will set dinner aside for when I head back home.

> Me: Not gonna make it back. You think you can make up two plates?

I hear Birdie making noises and pocket my phone. She doesn't need to worry or think I'm ruining my night by hanging with her.

"Birdie, you good, babe?" I hear the flushing of the toilet, the on and off of the water, yet she still isn't out. My mind plays the what-if game. What if she's in too much pain? What if she fell? What if she's breaking down and I'm not there to hold her? I'm not a damn fool. Birdie may have put up a good front for now. In the quiet of the night or when she thinks no one is around, that's when she'll break down.

"Yeah," she replies through the fucking door. I'm moving from my place, hand reaching out to turn the handle, when she appears in the doorway. "I went ahead and brushed my teeth. Sleep didn't come easy last night, and who knows if I'll wake up before morning." She lets out a yawn. She's so damn pretty, even with dark circles beneath her eyes, hair a tangled mess, and lips that are plump from her biting on them. The part that hits me in the solar plexus every damn time is that she has no damn idea how beautiful she truly is.

"Good idea. You need anything else? A glass of water?" She lets out another yawn, and I know it's time to get her in bed before she falls asleep standing up.

"No, I only need my bed and you in it with me." Her head lowers, hair cascading along the side of her face and covering her eyes from mine.

"You couldn't pry me away, Birdie." I tip her chin upward, needing to see the warmth of her eyes. We've still got it, and we're going to keep on until we take our last breath. Birdie may not have realized it, but she gave me the name of her attacker, and while the cops may be conducting their investigation, I'll be damned if I'm not doing my own.

"Thank you, Lane." She gives me what I want, and her gaze locks on mine.

"You got nothing to thank me for, Birdie. Now, let's get to bed." My arm wraps around her lower back, she places her head on my chest, and we make the short walk to her room.

In a perfect world, we'd be at my place, and her dog would be there with us. She wouldn't be dealing with the fallout of a dickhead, and she damn sure wouldn't be hurting. Then I wouldn't feel bad for eating her pussy while unknowingly adding to her injury. Birdie can say it didn't hurt, but I'm not stupid. I've broken and bruised my ribs before, and not from being beaten either. Nope, the rodeo shirt she's wearing is a testament not only to my younger years but today, too. I still ride in the local circuit during the spring and fall. Back then, I did it for extra money. Now, we do it as a sponsorship for the farm. The winnings we make now are donated to a charity Mom picks, and it's a damn good time.

"Mom never changed anything, so I hope you don't mind sleeping in a bed of flowers, literally."

"Get in bed, woman. I'm pretty sure my balls won't shrivel up and die for one night." I pull the comforter and sheets back. We didn't usually spend a lot of time here. It'd be kind of hard for Birdie to keep quiet. Plus, with my work schedule, it worked better with all the coming and going I did and still do.

"And I'm pretty sure they're blue," she jokes. I chuckle. She's not right and she's not wrong. Nothing kills a boner quite like seeing the woman you love hurting.

"Don't worry about my balls. You get better, and you can have them any way you want." Her eyes heat with desire. While she likes receiving, she's also a giver, and I know it's killing her to leave me hanging. Even though I give zero fucks about my cock right now.

"I'll hold you to that." Finally, once she's in the bed, head lying on her pillow, and I've got the covers up to her chest, I breathe easier. It's damn inconvenient when I can't even carry her to bed. "Where are you going?" she asks when I take a step back.

"Nowhere. I've got boots on. I can't necessarily climb into bed with them on." I step out of one, then the other, leaving them at the foot of the bed and out of the way in case Birdie needs to get up.

"Oh, okay." I move to the other side of the bed, pulling out my wallet, keys, and phone before climbing in beside her. I try my hardest not to jostle her, an impossible feat with her whole damn stomach covered in battle wounds.

"You think you can lie on your side?" I ask, my hand going beneath her neck. She used to lie in the crook of my arm, her head on my shoulder and a leg tossed on top of mine.

"Yeah, this side doesn't hurt." She settles in right where she belongs. Her hand rests over my heart, and I place mine on top. She settles in more, this time using me as her pillow. "Lane?"

"Yeah, baby?"

"I really missed you." Her words are muffled. She's already half-asleep.

"Missed you, too, Birdie." I don't tack on that had she not come home when she did, I was ready to get in my truck and hightail it to her. The only other option was packing my shit and moving. I'd already talked about the possibility to my parents and brothers. Dad, being Dad, got it. He hated seeing one of his boys leaving the family business, but if he were in my shoes, he'd be doing the same exact thing.

Birdie doesn't respond. A soft puff of air tickles my neck and throat, telling me she's already sleeping. I close my own eyes, unaware of the buzzing from the nightstand or the fact that both of our parents come into the room at one point. It seems both Birdie and I need sleep, this time with one another.

6

LANE

BIRDIE SLEPT WRAPPED in my arms the whole night, barely moving unless it was to get closer to my body. One time, I thought she was awake and asked if she needed medicine. She mumbled something I couldn't decipher and still can't figure out. As much as I tried to hold out on sleeping, it wasn't possible. Birdie being back made everything in my chest settle.

It didn't matter that when I did finally drag myself away from my woman, I was greeted by her mom in the kitchen. I figured she already knew I was there since my truck was parked in the driveway. Still, I grabbed my keys, phone, and wallet off Birdie's nightstand, trying to be as quiet as possible. Then I scooped up my boots to carry those as well.

Eleanor greeted me in the kitchen, a mug of coffee in front of her. She wasn't drinking it, only holding the ceramic flower cup. She looked at me, nodded, and said, "Thank you." I'm sure there's more to the story that Eleanor wanted to say yet didn't. Birdie thinks she's keeping shit under wraps, but anyone with two eyes and common sense can see what she's hiding. Eleanor didn't say a word when I told her I was grabbing a bottle of water and some pain relievers to put out for Birdie.

Now, I'm standing in the shower, the water running down my body, and I'm trying to breathe through the fact that my cock is refusing to go down. My balls ached all night, and my dick stayed hard the entire damn time. It's a wonder I'm not left with a permanent imprint of the zipper.

"Christ." My mouth hungers for another taste of Birdie, to feel the velvet clench of her pussy while I'm fucking her, and this time not with my mouth. My hand moves from the tile wall and wraps around the length of my dick. It's not going away anytime soon, and Birdie is out of commission. She may think she's up for my cock, but she isn't, especially not this week. The way I need her, it won't be soft and sweet like she deserves. It'll be fast and hard, and I won't stop until my cum is buried inside her.

Christ, the last time we were together, I pulled out. I didn't have a condom on hand, and she wasn't on birth control at the time. It took everything I had not to lose my load, to tie Birdie to me in a permanent way instead of letting her go off to college. I should have fucking done it, too. By the end of the summer, she would have been pregnant, probably pissed as hell, but then she wouldn't be black and blue either.

Immediately, a vision of Birdie comes to life. She's walking around barefoot, wearing my shirt without a stitch of clothing beneath. Her stomach is round with our child. The palm of my hand is slick with water, acting as lube, and the thought of her pregnant only makes my balls draw up tighter. My head drops forward as I imagine all the ways I'm going to take her the second she's not aching. On her back with her legs over my shoulders. My favorite would be with her on her hands and knees while I fuck my cock into her pussy and my thumb presses into the pucker of her ass.

"Son of a bitch." My knees buckle at the memory of how hard she comes on my cock when I play with her ass. It's out of this fucking world. I don't make it through any further. There's no time, and there's no way I can stop myself from coming. All night was a version of foreplay I wasn't prepared for. I squeeze my length, thumb pressing down on the head, and watch as cum shoots out of my body. A damn waste when it could be inside Birdie's mouth, her pussy, her ass, or even painted on her skin. I grab the soap, do a quick wash, and rinse. I've already been in here too long. It's time for me to get this show on the road. I turn the water off, grab my towel, do a quick dry off, and wrap the towel around my waist before stepping out of the shower.

"Fuck," I mutter, hearing my phone ringing in the distance. I stopped on my way home to look in on the cows, making sure everything was okay, checking the pregnant ones, seeing if any of them calved before I headed to my place. I'm sure a couple of the employees saw me even though none of them acknowledged me, which was probably a good thing, too.

My clothes were a wrinkled mess, and I still wasn't quite awake and coherent. So, if they did say something, chances are I wouldn't have any recollection of it. The somewhat of a downfall of them seeing me is them telling my parents where I'm at, and usually, the phone starts ringing off the hook. At least this time, I got a shower in first.

"Hello." I slide my thumb across the glass screen, hit the speakerphone, and take the phone with me.

"Hey, honey, you coming over to the house this morning?" Mom asks.

"Don't I always?"

"Well, yeah, but Eleanor said you spent the night, and I wasn't sure if you'd be bringing Birdie with you." I should have known better. Eleanor and my mom are as close as sisters these days.

"She's still asleep. I'm going to get some clothes on, eat some food, stop at the house, and then head back to Birdie's," I tell her while walking to the kitchen. When Mom and Dad gave each of us boys a few acres on the farm, it was with the intention they'd stay within the family. We'd build our house and pay taxes on it.

So far, there's only one brother who hasn't finished building his place. He's also two years older than me. Ryland is twenty-nine, a single dad, and the only reason he hasn't gotten his ass handed to him about taking as long as he has with the build of his place is my nephew, Case. He's only four months old and not sleeping through the night yet. We've all picked up where we could on Ry's house, but it's taking time. The ranch never rests, which makes it that much harder.

"Well, don't hog the poor girl. I haven't seen her in too long." I roll my eyes. Mom went with Eleanor on a few of their trips to Colorado.

"Catherine Johnson, leave the two of them alone. You saw her more than Lane did, and it's kind of hard to see someone who's asleep," Dad pipes in.

"Alright, alright. Your birthday dinner and dessert are in the fridge. Your spare key is under the mat now, too."

"About time," I hear Dad say in the background. My mother has a penchant for putting the phone on speaker, and today is no different.

"Hush, you, I'm glad our son is finally going after what he should have years ago. Though, I am glad he let Birdie spread her wings, so to speak. Anyways, come on over whenever. The pot of coffee is on, and breakfast is waiting." That's the last thing I hear before the phone line goes dead. At least this time, she hung up the phone before I heard something a son should never hear. One time, Mom thought she ended the call when she didn't. It was actually a Face-Time call, and I couldn't hit the end button fast enough. How Ryland still lives there is beyond me. As long as I don't have to see more than I already did, it's his problem. For now, it's time to make my cup of coffee, get dressed, and get this show on the road.

7

BIRDIE

"GOOD MORNING, SLEEPYHEAD," Mom greets me the next morning. I slept like a baby, probably because Lane stayed with me the whole night. I'm not sure I even moved most of the night. It wasn't until Lane kissed my throat, muttered he'd see me later, and placed the pillow he used in his place that I fell back to sleep.

When I woke up, the sun was shining brightly through the sheer curtains, and my nose was buried in Lane's pillow. The spicy scent of leather, cardamom, and Lane had my legs clenching together, which, of course, triggered the pain in my ribs and abdomen. The over-the-counter pain reliever had worn off sometime during my slumber, and I needed another dose, stat.

I rolled out of bed, grabbing the bottle of water that magically appeared on my nightstand, as well as the bottle of medicine. It didn't matter that my bladder was protesting. I tossed the pills back, chugged some water, and then went about my business. Secretly, I hoped it would kick in before now. Surprise, it didn't, and putting on a pair of sleep shorts never hurt so bad.

"Good morning. Sorry I slept so late." I glance at the clock on the stove, another shock hitting me when I realize it's nearly noon.

"Not a problem, honey. Lane said to call him when you woke up," Mom says with a smile. Meanwhile, I can feel the color blossom on my cheeks and neck. Jesus, I'm twenty-two, nearly twenty-three. I should not feel like I've been caught red-handed sneaking Lane into the house.

"Uh, about that." I bring the cup of coffee to my lips. It's so hot even with the cold creamer. The beauty of Mom having a pot of coffee on at all hours of the day, much like the Johnsons. My mom and their mom always have coffee, snacks, and then lunch ready for the employees who help them out. Speaking of, Mom is usually out in the field by this time, with a big straw hat on her head, a basket to collect flowers, and an apron to keep her extra cutters.

"I'm not worried about Lane sleeping in your bed. I figure it won't be long until you're living with him at his house. So I'll take you while I can." I nearly choke on my coffee. Which would suck, considering burning your throat is ten times worse than burning your tongue.

"Mom, I don't think that will happen. I have Rocky and Tully coming. She's moving to Arrowleaf and will be the new girl in town. What kind of friend would I be if I abandoned her as soon as she got here?" Alright, sue me. The idea of living with Lane is amazing. Falling asleep in his arms and waking up in them, well, it would be chef's kiss. Except I'm not even sure how to bring that up, and I've already said I wouldn't leave Tully.

"Honey, you act like Tully is going to move into the house. She's not, and you already know Lane isn't going to say no to you. My granddog is easy, small, behaves, and sleeps most of the day away." Yet again, Mom is right. She always is.

Tully is renting—yes, renting—because she refuses to take any type of handout whatsoever. The place she's staying at is on Mom's land. It was once a greenhouse. Mom said it was too pretty to house only her flowers, a relic of sorts. Mom renovated and turned it into a pretty cottage. She kept the original blueprint of the greenhouse since it was pretty big. The windows, sink, and anything she could repurpose, she did. They settled on a price over the phone two days ago, and everything was signed and sealed.

"I know. Ugh, we'll see. Is everything okay? You're usually not here during the day," I ask, still standing because it's currently the one position that doesn't hurt.

"As a matter of fact, it's not. Why don't you

sit down and talk to me." Mom's eyebrows lift to nearly her hairline. My stomach drops. *She knows.* God, how does she know? Lane wouldn't. He might go after my attacker, but what he wouldn't do is sit around, have coffee, and gossip about me to my mother. Yet I find myself doing exactly as she asks. There's no way to hide the wince or the fact that I'm taking my sweet time pulling the chair out, only to take a deep breath when my ass finally hits the seat.

"Mom." I look up. She's got tears forming in her eyes.

"Who? Who hurt my baby, and don't lie to me."

"Sherman Junior, my former boss's son." I swallow my own emotions. I did not want to have to talk about the situation again so soon. "How do you know?"

"Baby girl, there was a reason your dad left and never came back. I shielded you from it until I was strong enough to get help. Thankfully, you were young enough, or maybe you weren't. I prayed you didn't see or hear anything. I hoped to break the cycle. Yet here you are, coming home out of the blue, which I'm not mad about in the least. I saw the signs. It's why I didn't put up a fuss when you said no to going to Lane's birthday party." I push my coffee mug away, the caffeine sitting like lead in my stomach.

"I never knew, ever. I was going to tell you, swear. I've been trying to process it, mulling over how to even begin to explain this situation," I tell her truthfully. Only I'd have waited until there was a status update on my case and my body was somewhat healed.

"Were you dating him?" I shake my head vehemently while trying not to throw up in my mouth.

"No, I had never laid eyes on him a day in my life until he attacked me. I still don't know why he chose me. Maybe it was targeted, or maybe it was a case of him being born with a silver spoon in his mouth. You know, the type who's never heard the word *no* a day in their life." Mom stands up, the chair screeching across the tile floor.

"Please tell me you filed a police report. He didn't go further, did he?" She's white-knuckling the back of the chair. Suddenly, it all clicks, the reason Mom doesn't let anyone from the male species get close to her. My father did the worst besides beating her. He hurt my mom in a way that most don't overcome.

"Oh, Mom, you never told me." I bring my hand to my mouth, covering it to hide my trembling lips.

"And I wouldn't have. I'd have taken it to my grave. I also know when it happens, you need counseling, friends, family. So, you have to tell me, sweetheart. Did it go further?"

"No, I fought back hard enough, screamed loud enough that I was able to escape. The investigation is open. I'll be honest. I don't think Sherman Junior will get anything except a slap on his hand. They have the money and prestige from their name alone." I watch as Mom takes a deep breath and holds it in for a moment before exhaling.

"Thank Christ. As far as your attacker not getting what he deserves, I wouldn't be so sure about that. Lane Johnson looked like he was ready to slay all your dragons when he left this morning." And that's exactly what I'm afraid of. Lane won't do either of us any good if he's the one sitting behind bars while Sherman and his son get off scot-free.

8

LANE

"YOU MIGHT HAVE your work cut out for you, Lane." I step out of my truck when Eleanor is walking down the back steps. My parents and I talked for the better part of an hour, a lot longer than I was hoping to stay to visit. Mom wasn't having me rushing out the door, especially since I never made it back to her house last night. Meaning she didn't have the moment she hoped for when it came to celebrating my birthday. I'm not complaining. The last thing I wanted was a party to begin with. Dad could see I was chomping at the bit to get back to Birdie, and he finally told me to get out of there.

"I look forward to the fight she's going to give me." Eleanor smiles at my statement. I've already got a plan in place. Should Birdie choose to put up a fight with excuse after excuse, I'll pack her bags, throw them in the truck, and then somehow manage to get her in as well without hurting her.

"I'm glad. You know, when the two of you first got together, I was worried, worried you'd hold her back. I was wrong, Lane, and for that, I'm sorry."

"I appreciate the apology. It wasn't necessary, though. I'm guessing Birdie told you what happened in Colorado?" It's a fifty-fifty shot in the dark. Eleanor isn't dumb, and knowing my woman, she'll fold like a pretzel when it comes to her momma.

"You deserve it all the same." Eleanor takes a deep breath. "And yeah, she told me. I knew already. The quick change in plan, the fact Tully is coming, and Birdie showing up without her dog. It was all too telling. Though I'm going to let you in on a little secret. She was miserable in Colorado. She'd come home, realize you weren't here, and didn't want to stay. All this to say, take care of my baby." Well, shit, color me surprised. This whole damn conversation has my head spinning. I'll admit I was an idiot. No, I was a damn fool, tucking my tail and running when Birdie came home. That was all on me and knowing if I didn't, if she gave me the time of day, I'd do my hardest to convince her to stay. Eleanor doesn't need to hear that, and I bet she knows the truth anyway.

"You good with Birdie moving in with me?" I ask.

"Got no problem with that. You hoard my granddog, though, and we're going to have problems. I already know Birdie will find her way home every now and then since her best friend, Tully, is staying in the remodeled greenhouse." Makes sense. When Birdie lived here before going off to college, she didn't have a whole lot of friends, especially of the female variety. She thought it was a *her* thing. It absolutely wasn't her. It was the other girls and their insecurities. Birdie, with the pretty face, long hair, soft sway of her hips with each step, turns heads whenever she's nearby. She's oblivious to the attention she garners. She sees the good in everyone, wears her heart on her sleeve, and is willing to give the shirt off her back if it means someone needs it.

"I can't make any promises. He may like me more than you." I wink. Eleanor shakes her head.

"Go on in, but I promise you Rocky will be running back and forth between our properties, Rocky will end up here more than with you and Birdie. He knows who has the treats."

"Are you two seriously fighting over Rocky?" Birdie opens the door. She's still wearing my shirt from the night before, but her hair is now in a side braid, a few pieces hanging loosely, and she's got color to her face that she didn't have last night. There's also a fire in her eyes. Oh yeah, my woman is back in action.

"Your mom is. I already know Rocky will be wherever you are," I tell her as I take slow and measured steps, her eyes watching me in their entirety. It's going to be damn hard to keep my hands to myself while she heals. Especially when she bites her bottom lip.

"I'm going to the sunflower field. I have my phone on me, so don't worry. Good luck, Lane," Eleanor says.

"Later, Eleanor," I toss over my shoulder, my feet carrying me closer and closer to Birdie.

"Have a good day, Momma," Birdie says. My hands reach out to her hips, careful not to grip her too hard. It's then I notice she's wearing shorts. A damn shame I won't be able to get a look at her bare body. "Care to tell me what that was really about?" She pops a hip out, foot tapping, and she slowly crosses her arms over her chest. As if that's going to stop my gaze. The way her tits are now displayed through the thin cotton, nipples pebbled, and looking more beautiful than ever, it's clear I'll be jacking my cock for the foreseeable future, and this morning did nothing to settle the damn flesh down.

"Sure, let me go grab your bags, and I'll tell you all about it on the way home." The steps put us at eye level.

"Lane, I am home." She has no idea how wrong she is about that.

"No, Birdie, your home is with me. Where you lay your head down each night, I get all your good nights and all your good mornings." My lips graze along hers, shutting down anything she has to say. I coax her to open for me, my tongue sweeping along her lower lip, and when her hands move from her chest to my shoulders, I give her more. Birdie's body sways into mine, fingers digging deep like they always do when my mouth is on any area of her body, and I deepen our kiss. Our tongues stroke along one another's. I taste her sweetness with mine as her hands slide to the back of my neck and hold me there. It's not until she's breathless that I pull back. Her lips are wet from my mouth, her eyes are hooded, and I know there's no way I'd ever give her up without a fight.

"Lane." My finger covers her lips, stopping her before she starts.

"I'm not taking no for an answer. You don't want to say no. We both know this. Take my hand and come home, Birdie." I'd get on my knees and coax her into saying yes, using any means possible as long as she's with me.

"Fine, I'll go get my bags. They're already packed." She rolls her eyes. I shake my head.

"You're not getting your bags. You want to help, get your pretty ass in the truck." My hands slide down from her hips, cupping the cheeks of her ass and squeezing them.

"Okay." She moves closer, pressing her boundless tits along my chest, making me hiss out a breath.

"Babe, you're playing with fire."

"Maybe I want to be burned, Lane." When she moves to the side, I lose her, but I already know I'm gaining her for-goddamn-ever.

9

BIRDIE

"WOW, I love what you did with the place," I tell Lane with a hint of sarcasm when he opens the front door for me. I'm carrying absolutely zilch because he was adamant about me doing nothing but resting.

Memories assault me. I don't think there's a surface in this place we haven't touched in one form or the other. It's still as barren as when he first moved in. There's nothing on the walls, and the rich, dark-brown leather couch and chairs are in the same position. This means the couch is facing the fireplace, but what it's really focused on is the massive television. I guess there is one thing Lane changed because that was not as big the last time I was here.

"Thanks, it's called bachelor life. You know, the creature comforts are about all I need. A couch, a bed, a television or two, and food are the size of it. Hell, I barely need food. Ryland still lives at home, which means Mom and Dad always have their door open for breakfast and dinner. The only thing I worry about is lunch, and half the time, I'm too busy to stop and eat anyways." Lane drops my purse on the chair sitting in the corner, which is also facing the TV. What he doesn't do is drop my bags anywhere. Nope, he's got them firmly in his grasp. I shouldn't be surprised, except I am. He walks toward the hallway, his booted feet echoing off the hardwood floors.

"That'll be changing," I murmur under my breath. Lane taking care of me is so classically him, and well, now I'm in a position where I can do the same. Even if it's something small like packing his lunch and delivering it to him while he's working in an area. I'll need to use the side-by-side. Okay, fine, maybe I won't be able to do that right away. I can at least pack his lunch the night before or early in the morning. It's not like I have anything else to do, although I should be questioning how easily we've fallen back into how we once were.

"Did you say something?" Lane stops near the hallway, both of my bags in one hand, looking right at me.

"Nope, not a thing." I'm not ready to admit that I came home for more than one reason or the way Lane so easily offered up a solution with the job front.

"You good to walk, or do you need help?"

"I can walk," I reply. Unlike Lane, I take my shoes off. No way will I be the one responsible for scuffing his beautiful golden oak wood floors.

"Not fast enough." He sends a crooked grin my way as I kick off my shoes, well, slippers, rather. I had socks on, and much like now, back at my Mom's, he was impatient to get me here.

"Well, not all of us have your long legs, Lane Johnson." I roll my eyes and make my way toward him. He waits patiently like he always has. This man has a golden retriever personality like no other. Sweet, gentle, affectionate, easygoing, and, beyond all else, dependable. A characteristic I took advantage of when I was too young to realize what an amazing man Lane really is. He's also a good listener and is very observant. Fine, Lane Johnson is everything a person like me needs.

I'm stubborn to a fault, though I do like to blame that quality on my mother. I learned from the best. She'll do anything she can without asking for a lick of help. Eleanor Robertson would have to try it upside down, inside out, backward, and forward before she'd admit defeat.

Lane picks up his pace once I'm behind him, giving me a view of his broad shoulders, tapered waist, thick thighs, and round ass. The man has a dump trunk, and the funny part about it is he's not in a gym two hours a day, seven days a week. Oh no, his muscles are from working on the ranch, baling hay, riding horses, fixing fences, and the many other tasks he does on a daily basis.

"Like what you see?" I'm interrupted in my Lane daydream. I must have really been out of it. My bags are on the chair in the corner, and he's standing at the foot of the bed.

"You know I do." Last night wasn't enough. One time with Lane will never be enough. I'm more addicted to him today than I was when I left college. And don't get me wrong, the two of us may have been separated, a thought I don't want to think or talk about now and not ever, but it was always Lane Johnson for me.

"That I do. Wish like hell you weren't hurting, and I didn't have to continue with my day on the ranch." I almost pout at the thought of him leaving me already, except I can't. This is his job. He's not the one who's battered and bruised. Which means Lane won't allow me to do so much as ride along with him.

"Me too. I don't suppose I can talk you into letting me go with you?" He sits down on the edge of the bed, and I step closer, my knee nudging his until he opens them for me. I'm feeling a lot better after a full night of sleep and some medicine.

"No way in hell, baby." His hands slide up the back of my thighs. The blood in my body heats, my skin comes to life beneath his touch, and I'm going to have a hard time not begging him to take this a lot further.

"Fine. Leave me the Wi-Fi password. A lady of leisure I am not, so I may as well start figuring out how to make money." When everything went down, my job was the last thing on my mind. I have enough funds tucked away for a rainy day until I figure out what's next, and while I don't have a plethora of bills—thanks, Mom, for instilling a good ethic with money—the one credit card I have has a decent limit. I only use thirty percent of it at any given time and pay it off at the end of the month. My car may not be much, but there's no note on it, and it gets me from point *A* to point *B*. That being said, I still have day-to-day bills, like my cell phone, car insurance, and food. And while Lane is moving me into his house, I'd still like to have a job to contribute in some way.

"Look at the ranch's website, see what you think we should do. Mom hired someone, but it's not getting the traffic she expected it would. The phone is ringing off the hook for orders, and it'd be a lot easier if she didn't have to hold Case in one hand and the phone in the other." The Johnson Ranch is known for its beef cattle. They offer shipping for processed cuts of meat on the side.

"Are you sure?" Lane slides his hands up farther, cupping my ass, squeezing me while bringing me closer.

"Yep, already talked to her about it earlier this morning when I stopped by. It just so happened the phone had already started ringing and she was ready to turn the ringer off and pull her hair out. You'd be doing her a favor." My hands slide to his arms, feeling his muscles tighten as they continue their path until my wrists are on each of his shoulders, and my fingers are playing with his hair at the nape of his neck.

"Alright, I'll need the password, and I'll take a look and jot down notes. When you get back, we can ride over to the main house so I can chat with her." I can see the crinkle in his eyes. Lane is going to tell me no, and I'm going to hold my own. "Lane, you can't hold me captive. One phone call to your mom, and she'll come over and pick me up herself," I add for good measure.

My foot is ready to tap in annoyance, and then it all goes to shit when he says, "It's not that I'm locking you away in my house and throwing away the key. I only need a few days, just the two of us. My family is going to converge on you and take all your attention. Sharing isn't caring when it comes to you, Birdie." Well, I guess when Lane puts it that way, it's really sweet.

"Alright, I can see your side, but tomorrow evening? You still haven't celebrated your birthday with your family, and I feel awful about that."

"Maybe. Mom put food in the fridge. We'll have that tonight. See how you're feeling tomorrow and go from there. Think you can sit on my lap?"

"Yeah." My voice changes tones, going from a *don't back down* stance *to I'd get on my knees right now if you'd allow me*. Instead, I use Lane. One knee goes to the outer edge of his hip, and he helps me until I'm sitting in his lap.

"Fuck, Birdie, the next time I have you like this, we won't have a stitch of clothing on, and you're going to ride my cock." My center clenches, my eyes go hazy, and I'm lost in what I knew could very well happen right now if only Lane would allow it.

"Please." I slide closer until my pussy is on top of his hard, thick cock.

"Soon," Lane groans before his mouth meets mine and he shuts up any other pleas I could possibly bring up.

10

LANE

"BIRDIE, I'M HOME!" I walk through the door hours later. A door that is unlocked. I'll have to change that. I close and lock the front door for the evening. The last thing I need is one of my brothers showing up unannounced, barging through the door, and seeing Birdie naked.

"In the bedroom!" she calls back. I take my boots off at the door, not wanting to track dirt through the house. Birdie would take it upon herself to sweep, vacuum, and mop, and that ain't gonna happen anytime soon.

Today, when I left, I knew she'd be doing some work. What I didn't expect was her to unpack everything already. I'm not going to complain unless she wore herself out. It's nice to see our stuff mixed in together. There still isn't much on the walls, but there are frames placed here and there.

One of the pictures is from years ago. She's on the tailgate of my truck, arms wrapped around my neck, legs surrounding my hips. I'm leaning back into her. One of those moments, she came over with lunch. Mom was around and snapped the picture of the two of us smiling at the camera. I never did get a copy. Glad Birdie did. And with the way it's framed, I'm thinking it's been like that all along.

My walk shows me she's added a few other things, like a couple of vases, one on the coffee table, another on the counter, and I know exactly where the flowers came from. My woman is a lot like her momma. The Robertson women love the vibrant colors of Ellie's fields, and it shows in both of our houses.

"Whatcha doin', Birdie?" I ask as I walk down the small hallway. I'd honestly expected her to be at the kitchen table or in the living room, still working the day away. Truthfully, I'm glad she's not. I'd much prefer her in bed, resting. I know the probability of that happening wasn't likely.

"Just got out of the shower. Now I'm looking for something to wear." The breath leaves me. She's standing in the closet, wearing nothing but a towel. Birdie's hair is down. Wet. And there are still a few droplets of water sliding down her chest when she turns to look at me.

"Birdie," I groan. My hand grips the back of the neck of my shirt, pulling the cotton of my tee over my head. "Drop the towel, baby." I was going to wait until she was completely healed, not even so much as a bruise on her body. I can't. The need to take her is too deep. I'm not sure why I ever thought I could hold back. Last night should have told me that. Birdie consumes my every waking need, and I don't care if I have to be gentle. I'll make her stay perfectly still while we both chase our orgasm.

"Drop your jeans, Lane," she counters.

"Fuck yeah." I bring my foot up, sliding one sock off after the other. Birdie is waiting on me, keeping the status quo, but the second my hand pops open the button of my jeans, she lets the towel go, and while, yes, her torso is a mottled mess of colors, Birdie is fucking beautiful. "Gonna need you on the bed, Birdie, or I'm gonna take you against the wall." My jeans drop to the floor, and I step out of them.

"I have no problem with that idea. Too bad I know you won't." She takes one slow step at a time as she walks toward me, the softness in her body and the slow sway of her hips captivating me with each step she takes.

"You gonna have a problem when I fuck my cum inside your bare pussy while you're not on birth control?" Once she's within reaching distance, the tip of my finger slides down the slope of her neck.

"Nope. I'm pretty sure we've wasted enough time." Her hand wraps around my length, and that's all I can take. The last time I had her, condoms were involved for the most part, except that first and the last time. I wasn't imagining it to go that far, so I didn't have a condom on me. She was a virgin, and feeling her skin to skin, it took all I had to pull out well before I was ready to come inside her.

"You got that fuckin' right. I can't wait to watch your body grow with our child in your belly." Her eyes turn to molten desire, her nipples pebble harder, her thighs squeezing together. "Need you on the bed." I step back, losing her hand on my cock.

"Okay, Lane." The back of her body is just as gorgeous as her front, and damn if I don't want my face buried between her thighs as I use my mouth on her from behind.

"On your back, baby. I'm going to do the work, and you're going to have to stay very still. Can you do that for me?" My hand takes the place hers was only moments ago, jacking my cock as I follow her. Fuck, her ass. I can't wait to feel the tight clench of it around my length while I fuck her pussy with my fingers, watching how hard she flies apart with me taking her ass.

"I can get on my back, Lane, but I'm not making any promises about staying still," she tosses over her shoulder. There isn't a wince or so much as a tinge of pain around her eyes. She must really be feeling better. She's probably staying up on pain relievers, too. All I've gotta do is make sure I don't hurt her too much. It fucking sucks because when it comes to Birdie, I lose all sense of control.

"Woman, you going to make me deny you my dick?" I watch as she lies on the edge of the bed, spreading her legs open and looking in my direction.

"You wouldn't. I know you, Lane. You talk a big game, but you'd never do something like that. We'd both be aching with the need to have one another." She licks her lips. Birdie is right, which is why I quit pretending I'm going to hold back. The second I'm in front of her, she widens her thighs, and I move closer.

"You're right. You gonna be able to wrap your legs around me, Birdie?" I'm unsure how to handle her, wanting to tread carefully but still give her a damn say.

"Like this?" Her legs hook behind my back, ankles locking in place and making me move closer.

"Fuck yeah. Not sure how long this is gonna last. It's been a long fucking time, baby." I guide my cock to her glistening cunt, wetting the tip, trying to hold back from slamming deep inside of her. Shit, the way I'm going, I do that, and I'll come right away, and I'll be damned if I do that to her.

"Same, Lane. So please don't make me wait." Her eyes close, eyelashes splayed across her cheeks and lush lips pressed together. My own continue their path, taking in the red flush along her skin, the way her tits are moving with each deep breath.

"Son of a bitch." The velvet clutch of her pussy bears down on my cock, and I'm barely inside her. My mouth waters, trying to figure out where I want it first— her nipples, her skin, or her lips.

"Lane." My hips press deeper, her legs wrap around me tighter, and I'm forced to go down on my elbows, or I'll give too much of my weight. I frame our bodies on either side of her head, coming face to face, and now I know where my mouth is going to land first.

"God, Birdie, you feel good, too good." I pull back sparingly, unable to leave too much of her wet heat, and then I thrust back inside. Her hands wrap around my biceps, fingers pressing into the skin as she lifts her hips, trying to get me as deep as possible. While I want nothing more than to fuck my cock into her as hard, fast, and deep as I can, the possibility of hurting her is still at the forefront of my mind.

"Lane William Johnson, quit fucking holding back. I'm not made of fine china. You're not going to hurt me. You're going to piss me off, and then I'll just take care of myself." This woman, I should have known she wouldn't fight fair. Her hand comes off my arm, and I know exactly what Birdie is after.

"You so much as touch your pretty pussy, I'm

going to roll you over and spank that ass, baby, then you won't be coming either. I'll spank you red, jack my cock, and paint your ass with my cum. You wouldn't want that. Depriving us both of coming together, hmm?" Her hand stops on her lower abdomen, and through my talking, I've slowly ramped up my speed. Her tits bounce, her eyes are having a harder time staying open, and her cunt clamps down on my cock.

"Lane, don't stop. Please." Her hand moves away from her body, going back to my bicep, where it fucking belongs. I slide a hand to her outer thigh, pulling it up higher, opening her farther.

"I swear, Birdie, this is everything. You're everything." Gone is my attention on making sure she isn't hurting. In its place is the need to make Birdie mine, to fuck my baby into her body, and to make her realize she'll always be mine.

"I'm close, oh god." Fuck yeah, she is. I can feel her cunt ripple along my length, feel her clenching, and I can feel her pulling me right along with her.

"Fuck yeah, you are. Take me with you, Birdie." I lift her leg up even more until it's on my shoulder, my mouth finding the inside of her ankle and grazing it with my lips. I get the show of the century. Birdie's head falls back, neck arching, body glistening with sweat, and she's shaking. The orgasm takes hold of her, and she moans out my name as she comes undone. My body can't hold back any longer. I piston my hips harder and faster, ready to, with any luck, fuck a baby inside of her.

"Birdie." I rock my hips, head tipping back, balls drawing tight, and my cum jets deep inside of the only woman I've ever loved.

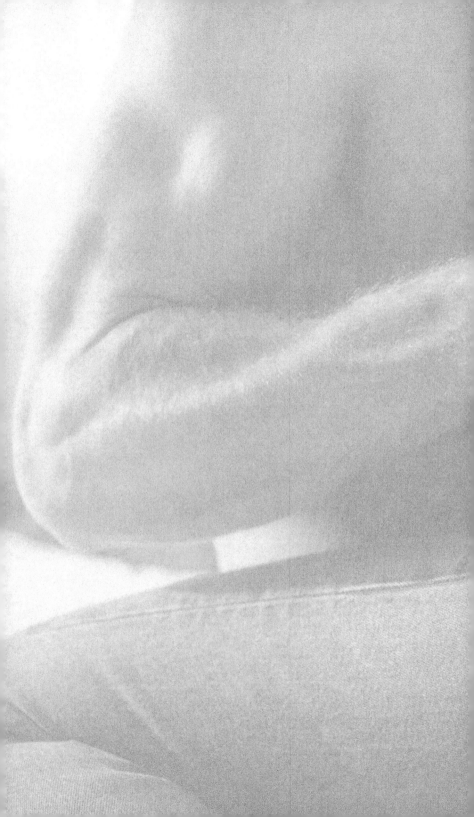

11

LANE

"WHERE ARE YOU GOING?" Birdie asks as I untangle myself from her body, the covers, and eventually the bed. I was hoping she'd sleep through me getting up. Fat lot of good that did.

"Gotta make a call and start my day. Sleep, yeah?" The lids of her eyes open for a minute before closing as I run the tips of my fingers along her forehead, moving her soft tendrils of hair away from her face. Birdie naked in my bed is what dreams are made of, and while I hate the marks on her body, it's a testament to her surviving the bullshit she's been through. I probably shouldn't have taken her up on her advances, but there's only so much a man can take. And one time wasn't enough. After I had her flat on her back, not allowing her to move in the slightest, doing all the work even when she tried to lift her hips to meet my thrusts, the last time was with us facing one another, she on her side, leg hiked up over my hip. That time, keeping her still was impossible. When we were finished, I went into the bathroom, grabbed a washcloth, and doused it with warm water while grabbing the aspirin I knew Birdie would need. I cleaned her, placed a kiss on her bare pussy, made sure she took her medicine, then took care of the washcloth before climbing back into bed beside her.

"Don't take too long. Wanna snuggle." Since the second I came through the door yesterday, Birdie hasn't left my side except to eat or use the bathroom. I'm not complaining. I like the fact that she's as addicted to my presence as I am hers.

"You got it." I've only left her long enough to do the bare necessities on the farm and talk to my brother Lawson. He's the oldest of the bunch of us brothers, and he also has a friend who can help me out with a delicate situation. I watch as Birdie sinks back into the pillow, staying where I am until I know she's back asleep. The last thing I want is her finding out what I'm doing or who I'm going after. She's been adamant about letting the police do their thing, and that's fine. They can, but that doesn't mean I can't push the process along with a call to Fletch. He used to live here after his stint at the academy but transferred back to Georgia a while ago back to work in another division. Then he moved again, hating being undercover and in the bigger city. Now he's working in a more rural area, his hometown, much like here in Arrowleaf, only he's a detective in Peachtree.

I grab my black sweatpants off the chair, slide them on, and go to my nightstand to pick up my phone. Then I make my way out of the bedroom, pulling the door behind me but leaving it open just a crack. I don't want Birdie to think I'm hiding something from her, even if I'm bending the truth a smidge. Which is why I'm taking this to the back porch, not even bothering with a cup of coffee first. If I don't get this taken care of, there's no telling how long it'll go on with that piece of shit roaming the streets.

I unlock my phone and scroll through my contacts until I land on Fletch's number. My thumb hits dial, and I put the phone up to my ear while unlocking the back door. It's early in the morning here, which means Fletch is a couple of hours ahead in the day. He's probably already been at the station for most of the morning while we're about to start our day, fucking time zones can be a bitch.

"This is Fletch," he answers the phone, probably not bothering to look at his display.

"Hey, it's Lane. Lane Johnson." Fletch and Lawson are closer in age and were thick as thieves for a while. The two of them would raise hell any way they could, at the rodeo, at the bar, and even on the farm. . That all changed once they hit twenty-one. Fletch stopped wandering and went to the police academy. And while Lawson had a job, he became more goal focused. At least that's what Mom and Dad tell the younger brothers, probably to keep us in line.

"It's been a minute. How are things going your way?"

"Good, Birdie's home. How about yourself?" He keeps in touch with us enough to know the ins and outs of what's happening.

"I heard. Bet you're happy." He lets out a chuckle.

"You could say that. Lawson talk to you lately?" I'm sure he's got shit to do, which could be said for myself.

"A couple of weeks ago. Everything okay?" I hear the creak in his chair as if he's sitting up and taking notice.

"For the most part. This is about Birdie. I was wondering if you could take a look into an investigation." Fletch lets out a breath of relief.

"Sure, what am I looking at?"

"You know Birdie's full name. Her boss's son attacked her this week. She made a statement and is pressing charges. Birdie came back home and has yet to hear anything back. Apparently, this Sherman guy is well-to-do and can grease palms of the law. You catch my drift? Birdie, being Birdie, wants to put it behind her, but in the meantime, it's her who's out of a job and it's her who has to deal with recovering."

"How bad of a recovery are we talking?"

Fletch, like most men, our minds go to the worst case possible. I know mine sure as fuck did once I saw the bruises. It took me a minute to realize she wouldn't have let me eat her if that were the case.

"She wasn't raped." Saying that word alone has my gut roiling. "Bruised rib or two. Torso suffered the same fate. If she hadn't gotten away when she did, I have no reason to think he wouldn't have taken it a step further."

"Thank fuck for small favors. I'm willing to bet this isn't his first rodeo in this scenario. I'll do some digging. See what I can find out. I've got a buddy who works in Colorado. He may know more about the guy than we would," Fletch explains.

"You're not wrong about that. Still eats at my gut every time she winces or makes a sudden movement."

"Text me the details. It'll be easier to plug in the information and go from there. Everything else good at the ranch?"

"I'll send it now." I put him on speakerphone to send him the name, city, and date the incident occurred. "Yeah, they're good. Mom is happier than a pig in shit with Case living under their roof. Though I think Ryland is probably ready to hurry the process of moving out along."

"I bet. Gotta be tough going through this while having your parents watching the whole time. Good, bad, or indifferent," Fletch says what we all see with our two eyes.

"Yeah, it's been fun, that's for sure."

"Alright, I got your text. I'll let you know as soon as I know something. It was good to hear from you, Lane, even though it was bad news." Yeah, he's calling me out for not staying in touch like I should be.

"I appreciate it more than you know." We hang up with one another. My forearms meet the railing, and I bend at the waist to take a deep breath. The other half of my heart and soul is in my bedroom. I should be shaking this shit off and getting back in bed with her like she asked. Today is going to be the day Eleanor, my mom, dad, and brothers are going to expect us to come up for air. I also promised Birdie I wouldn't try and keep her from going and doing. In order to keep that promise, I'm going to have to share my woman. Fuck, do I hate the sound of that.

"Lane, what are you doing out here? You're usually on the front porch." She's right. This deck is also the farthest away from the master bedroom. The way my house is set up, the front porch has the best views.

"Had to make a call." I stand up, and when I do, I feel her arms wrap around my stomach. Her front is plastered to my back, and I lock her hands in place with one of mine.

"That doesn't sound ominous at all." She places a kiss on my spine, and I turn my body so I can wrap her up instead of her wrapping me up.

"It's all good, baby." I kiss the crown of her

head, breathing her in. "I figure today our time in hiding is up. My family is bound to converge on us, and I'd rather they don't barge through the door. Which reminds me, I need to change the damn lock. There are too many keys floating around as it is."

"You're acting awfully put out, considering the fact that I do need to speak to your mom about the website. I also need to sit down with my own. Her website needs work, too, you know?" She tips her head up, eyes filled with laughter and happiness. Thank Christ. It killed me to see her looking sad when I first walked through the door.

"Doesn't mean I have to like it." This time, she does laugh, and it's me who swallows it down with a kiss. If I'm going to lose her for most of the day, I may as well get a taste that will last me a while.

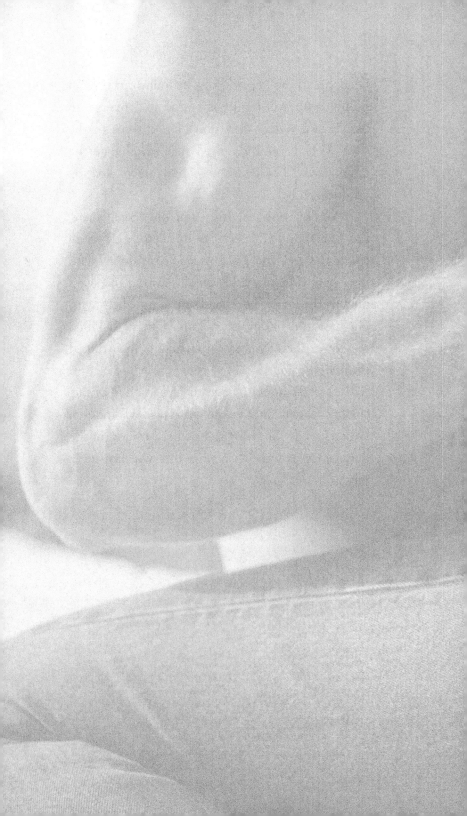

12

BIRDIE

"PLEASE TELL me you're almost here?" I ask my best friend once I'm out of bed for the day. I miss her and Rocky terribly. She should have already been here, but hiring a moving company at the last minute proved to be harder than we thought.

"Not so much. Am I going directly to your mom's or Lane's?" If we were on a FaceTime call, she'd be wiggling her eyebrows, doing some weird kind of thrusting with her hips. Clearly, she has an older brother.

"Mom's. Lane is working, and I'm feeling much better. I swear he'd wrap me in bubble wrap if he could." I was surprised to find him on the porch this morning before work. He's usually in the kitchen or out front. There was something heavy on his mind, a subject Lane wouldn't share with me, and while it made me second-guess our relationship, I had an internal debate with myself. I thought about all the moments I've had with Lane, the way he put his birthday party and birthday on hold to come to me. How he's taken care of me since the moment his eyes landed on mine. Then there's before I left, when I gave myself to him in every way possible. He's my first love, my first partner, my first everything. And when I went to college, my heart stayed here in Arrowleaf with Lane. So I took a deep breath while he held me, and I got my thoughts unscrambled. My heart is Lane Johnson's, and his heart is mine.

"From the stories you've told me and the texts you've been sending, I wouldn't mind a cowboy like him. Tell me again, how many brothers are there?" The sip of coffee I'm taking goes down the wrong way, and I almost spew it all over myself and the kitchen counter. Today, I'm able to sit on the barstool without wincing in pain. My ribs and sternum are barely noticeable. My pussy, though, that's another story. Lane tried his hardest to keep me still, to keep me from pulling him over the edge with me, but there was no way that was happening. The first time, yes. The second time, absolutely not. My body craved his, and once Lane allowed himself to let go, it was a thing of beauty. I kept my eyes open the entire time he came deep inside me. Watching his powerful thrusts, his muscles tightening, his sweat coating our skin, the way his head tipped back, his body locking up. And how he breathed my name when he came deep inside me. My core clenches, wanting to relive the moment, yet knowing today is going to be busy for both of us. Maybe Lane keeping me to himself wasn't such a bad idea after all.

"There are six Johnson brothers all together. Lane is obviously off-limits. From oldest to youngest, you have Lawson, Trey, Dean, JW, Ryland, and Lane. Their ages start at thirty-seven and end at twenty-seven." Mrs. Catherine and Mr. Russel surely did a lot in a ten-year time span.

"And do all of them have Lane's looks?" Thank goodness she's asking me about this while Lane isn't around. He'd lose his shit if he heard me talking about another man, let alone his brothers. The one thing about these Johnson men, they love hard and protect harder. They also do not share what's theirs, especially Lane. I know he let me go for a reason. I also know he was never home when I was for the same exact reason. It sucked, but our love for one another ran deep enough to weather the storm.

"Well, first of all, Lane is the hottest, but all of the Johnson brothers are good-looking. I can't say for sure how their personalities are since coming home this time around. Lane quite literally kidnapped me the day I came home and has sequestered me away at his house." Yes, I know it's only been a couple of days, but other than my mom, it's only been the two of us since I parked my car in the driveway.

"And you're complaining?" Tully snorts her reaction, and then I hear him. I hear my baby boy doing a yip in the background.

"Not at all. Okay, for real this time. How much longer till you're in Arrowleaf?" I'm still in Lane's shirt, my hair is a knotted mess, and I need to do a few things around the house. Then there's the fact I'll have to walk to my mom's, or I could make a call to either my mom or Lane. Hmm, I really need to think this through.

"Um, considering we've had to make several stops after the amount of coffee I've consumed, it's safe to assume I won't be there till around lunchtime. Rocky and I are also enjoying each pit stop by stretching our legs, aren't we, boy?"

"Fine. If it must take you that long, I suppose I'll clean up around here and head to Mom's. I'll make sure lunch is ready. Promise me you'll call when you need to?" I make it sound like a question. Tully knows it's more of a *you better, or else I'm going to be pissed.* She's been there for me. Now it's time for me to be there for her.

"Yes, mother hen, I will. Between you and my mom, I don't think I've had the chance to listen to a whole chapter of my audiobook."

"We love you, so suck it up, buttercup." I wish audiobooks did it for me like they do for Tully. She can read on her e-reader or listen to an audiobook and soak up every single detail. I'm more of a paperback girlie, and on the rare occurrences a thick book is too much to carry, I'll pull out my own e-reader. Usually, when the latter happens, I'm in bed for the night, my eyes are tired and heavy, then the next thing you know, my face is feeling the gravity-forced e-reader bopping me in the face. I get annoyed and vow to only read paperbacks until the next time.

"Yeah, yeah, smooches. We love you, and we'll see you soon." I start to respond, but this bitch of a best friend of mine hangs the fuck up on me. I mean, sure, sometimes I'll extend the conversation on a different subject. It's a habit of mine and usually ends up being a tangent about nothing. Still, it would have been nice to say bye.

"Freaking brat." I place the phone on the counter, pick up my cup of coffee again, and take a sip. I've got a decision to make. As much as I wouldn't mind walking to my mom's, even I know it might be a bit too much on my body. There's always the side-by-side in Lane's garage I could take. Maybe I'll leave a note and tell him where I am. I shake my head. Nope. I'm not trying to be denied an orgasm. He'd do it, too. Especially given that even I know my body is still healing. A bumpy ride would be bad, which also means walking that far is definitely a no-go. I'm dialing his number without another thought. This way, I'll get to steal a kiss or two from him in the middle of the day.

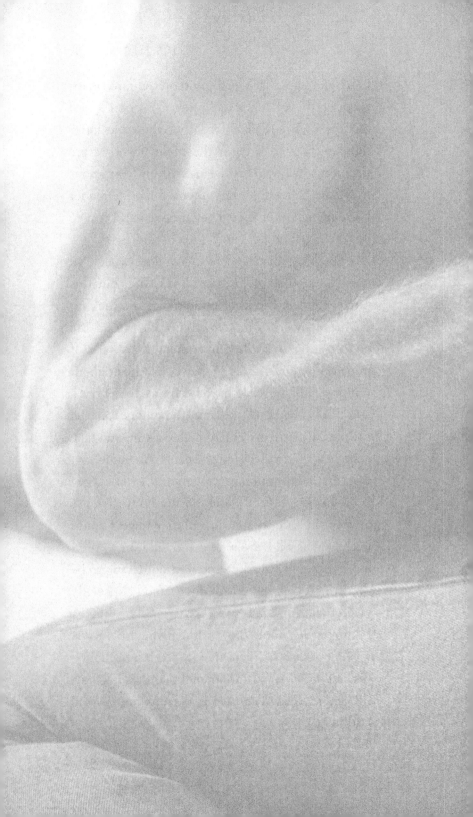

13

LANE

"BIRDIE, YOU DECENT?" I open the door, noticing it's unlocked, and I've yet to do a thing about it. Kind of hard to complain to Birdie to lock the door when I haven't even discussed the issue of my family potentially barging in. The very least I can do is gather all the fucking spare keys that are circulating around the ranch. Today, I'll take care of changing the lock after I drop Birdie off at her mom's. As it is, I've got Juniper with me, our ranch nurse. Even though she's of the female species, no fucking way am I going to bring someone in our house with Birdie only wearing my shirt and nothing else.

"Yes, do you think I walk around the house naked?" she yells through the house, making an appearance from the hallway. The air leaves my lungs when I see her. It's clear as day that a few days of rest have done her body good. Birdie has her hair in another side braid, and she's wearing a tank top, jean shorts, and a flannel. My girl turned into a woman during her time away, and you can take the girl out of the country, but you can't take the country out of the girl. On her feet, she's wearing the same worn-down cowboy boots.

"I wouldn't be opposed."

"You're just like your brother. Move out of the way. I've got about ten minutes before another one of you cowboys does something stupid, and I need to patch them up," Juniper inserts with a snort.

"Birdie, this is Juniper. She's going to take a look at your ribs." Birdie is rolling her eyes before I can finish my sentence.

"Will this appease you enough for me to take the side-by-side to Mom's, or will you drive me over, and I can drive my car back?" Her eyebrows shoot up near her hairline. This is a goddamn test, I can feel it, and I'm not stepping in the mound of horse manure if I can help it.

"That depends on what Juniper has to say."

"Hey, Birdie, I'm Juniper, but I go by Juni most of the time. Do you mind if I take a look at what we're working with? I promise to be fast." She steps right into nurse mode. She's small but mighty. The hands around the ranch know not to fuck with her, or she'll fuck back harder. It's also why Lawson has a hard-on the size of Texas for her.

"Nope, not at all. What do you need me to

do?" I walk toward where the two of them are standing.

"Lift your shirt. I won't be able to see how bad the bruising is internally unless we do X-rays. And since you only had them a few days ago, from what Lane told me, it's safe to assume they'll be about the same. I'd suggest in the next week or so, we can do them again."

I listen to their conversation while watching as Birdie lifts her shirt. It still eats me up inside to see her bruised. In my head, I know she was lucky. I know she'll heal, and I know it'll take time. My heart is another story entirely. I'm ready for the process to hurry up. I can't very well leave her alone for a day or two, driving to Colorado to take out the trash when she's still dealing with everything. Plus, I'm still waiting to hear back from Fletch on any details he can gather.

"Yeah, I'd rather not have more X-rays." We're only a few feet away from one another, but when our gazes lock, Birdie's cheeks blush with color, and she looks down at where she's holding her shirt up for Juni. I get it now. Boy, do I fucking get it. Instead of seeing the blue, purple, and yellowish haze on her body, all I'm seeing is her round with our child. Now more than ever, I want that to happen. Each time I've taken Birdie, there's been no pulling out, and she's not on birth control, so there's a very good chance she'll be pregnant sooner than later.

"I don't blame you. Okay, this may hurt a bit. I'm just trying to get the lay of the land. Is there any chance you can send me the medical records?" Juniper presses down in an area that must tweak Birdie.

"Yeah, I can do that. I'll call tomorrow unless you need them today?" There's a twinge of pain in her voice. I keep my eyes glued to her the entire fucking time, ready to call a halt to this entire damn thing, even though this was my idea.

"Tomorrow is fine. We're not doing an X-ray anytime soon. When we do, we'll have a comparison to make sure everything is healing correctly." Juniper finishes her assessment, and Birdie's shirt falls back down.

"Alright," she responds.

"Everything looks good from what I can see and feel. I'd suggest not taking the side-by-side. You can drive and do everything else as usual, though." She looks over her shoulder. "As long as she's not hurting, she'll be fine." Birdie smirks, knowing she's getting her way.

"Fine," I grunt. Now I'm really going to have to share my woman.

"These damn cowboys, they pout more than any toddler I've ever seen before," Juniper replies. I haven't even said anything, yet I'm getting shit. Lawson must have pissed her off good and well today. Then again, when doesn't he?

"Thank you, Juniper. I appreciate you coming out here."

"No problem. Whenever you get the records, let me know. It goes without saying I hope the person who did the damage receives it back tenfold. I'm heading out unless you need anything else?"

"Nope, we're good. I'm going to take Birdie to her mom's, then get back to work myself." I've been doing what has to get done, but going the extra mile like I usually do? Absolutely fucking not.

"Yes, thank you. Lane, move your butt. My best friend and my dog will be at Mom's before I am." When Birdie called me to give me four options, counting each of them, I knew Juniper was coming back to the house with me. I didn't like a single option except one. Birdie walking to her mom's was a hard no. Taking the side-by-side was a hard fucking no. Calling her mom for a ride wasn't bad, but still a no. That left me taking Birdie and her driving back home. It didn't make me clench my teeth nearly as bad as the others. Still, I wanted to make sure she wasn't doing too much too soon, which is why I brought Juniper.

"Come on, we'll drop Juni off on our way to your mom's."

"I can walk. In fact, I think I may need to. It was great meeting you, Birdie. I'm sure I'll see you around."

Juniper walks toward the front without

saying anything else. I'd like to say I'll figure out what Lawson did to irritate her, but truth be told, I've got more important matters on my hands. Like kissing my woman and reminding her I'll be here when she comes home.

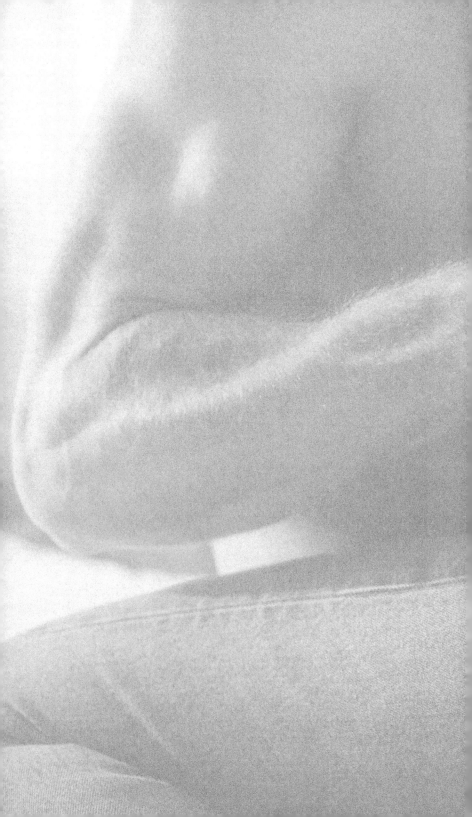

14

BIRDIE

"TULLY! ROCKY!" I run out of my mom's house, well, as much as I can without hurting myself, so it's more like a fast walk. Mom is hot on my heels, and I bet this is how she felt each time I came home.

"Birdie, don't you trip. Lane will kick my butt," she says behind me. Is everyone afraid of my man except me? I mean, he's got a big bark, but the only bite I get is when he's in bed with me. My breasts currently feel his marks with each movement of my body, the lace bra doing absolutely nothing to help matters either.

"Come to Mommy, Rocky." I squat down as Tully opens the door. Is my dog my pride and joy? Absolutely. Did my best friend pack everything we'd both need into her massive SUV and drive to my hometown, restarting her whole life because of me? Yes. Do I feel guilty? Well, kind of. I also know Tallulah doesn't do a damn thing she doesn't want to. Oh, how I hated leaving the two of them behind, but another chance encounter with my attacker was the biggest worry of all. Now, our two-bedroom apartment is being packed by movers, and she's here to stay. Everyone needs a Tully in their life. I only hope I can one day return the favor of being a great friend to her as well.

"Glad to see he gets the attention like normal," Tully says, stepping out of her massive SUV. Rocky all but attacks me, not in a mean way, in an excited, *he can't sit still* kind of way. I drop to my butt with a wince. The pain is nothing when his tongue comes out to lick me, his version of giving kisses. He's jumping around, prancing on two feet, his little booty wiggling back and forth in excitement.

"Well, once I'm licked to death, I'll be sure to hug you, too." I look up from my place on the ground. My best friend is standing with my mom. Mom has her arm wrapped around Tully, and while my friend has the look of yuck written all over her face, Mom looks like she's trying to hide her laughter.

"No, I'm good. I had a shower already. Pretty sure I don't need another until after we off-load this stuff." I pick myself up off the ground, then do the same for Rocky until he's under my arm on my good side, and walk toward Tallulah.

"You think carrying him around is a good idea?" Mom asks.

"Probably not. I've missed him, though." I shrug my shoulders, and his cute little face looks up at me. Rocky has one blue eye and one brown eye, and it's hard to resist anything he asks when he looks as cute as he does.

"I'm going to laugh when Rocky pees all over you," Tully says.

"Fine, I'll put him down. Do you want to visit or drive over to your place and get you somewhat unpacked until the movers bring the rest?" Tully's done a lot, fixing my problems. Picking up the pieces of my mistakes, the consequences so dire she had to make one decision after the next. I could barely move after the trip to the hospital visit, as well as talking to the police officers who were assigned to my case.

My mind couldn't keep up, and my body was ready to give out. And when it was time for me to head home, I could barely move, much less pack in my tiny car what she was able to fit in hers. Where I was living in Colorado, I could walk to most places. College, the grocery store, and work. Tully has a big SUV. She was more confident driving her vehicle around the crowded town than I would ever be. So she took it upon herself to load what I needed for a few days, then proceeded to pack what she could in her vehicle and drive here.

"I love you, and I want to visit with you. I also

want to unpack, take a hot-as-hell shower, collapse in bed, and sleep for the next twenty-four hours." Ugh, the guilt that rolls through my stomach. I can see how tired she is. Her clothes are a rumpled mess, her hair is in a ponytail that is falling down, and she looks like she's been mainlining coffee for two days straight.

"Alright, let me grab my phone and keys. Mom, you wanna drive her truck to the greenhouse?"

"Sure, talk about me like I'm not here," Tallulah says, but she's already walking toward the passenger side of the car.

"Get inside and call Lane and one of his brothers. Neither of you girls should be off-loading all of this. Plus, your stuff will need to be moved to Lane's," Mom tells me before bending down and picking up Rocky. He was jumping up on his short little legs to get her attention. My boy refuses to be left out at any given time.

"I feel like we should call Ms. Catherine, too, but I don't want to overwhelm Tully on her first day here. She's already done so much." Mom takes a step closer, looks over her shoulder, and I do the same. Tallulah's door is open, allowing the sun to give me a clear view of just how much she's packed. There are boxes and bags stacked, and it's not like her vehicle is compact. I'm talking three rows, the last being up, and there's still a massive-ass trunk.

"Nope, I'll call her later today, and if she

can't find a job, I know a rancher or two who could use her area of expertise."

"Well, that's probably for the best since her head is tipped back and her mouth is open in the passengers seat. Tully is well and truly out like a light. As for her taking freebies, good luck. I've mentioned her opening up a veterinary office, and that was the one thing that sparked her interest. The only problem with it would be the initial cost and the time it'll take to build up her patient list." Honestly, Tully could do it. She's the hardest worker and is so passionate about her work.

"We'll cross that bridge when we get to it. Now here, take Rocky, and don't be too long. The girl needs to get horizontal, much like my daughter did when she came home."

"I don't know what you're talking about," I tease, putting Rocky beneath my arm again. This time, he's more content and places his head on my chest before letting out a tired yawn.

"Sure you don't," she retorts.

"I probably get it from someone else I know." Stubbornness runs in our blood a mile long, and there's no sign of it stopping. Mom heads toward Tully, and I start my short walk toward the house. Once I'm there, I head to the kitchen counter, where I had placed my keys as well as my phone. Lane only left a couple of hours ago, and I feel horrible for asking him to stop his day yet again, except I know what will happen if I don't.

I pick up my phone and send him a text. He's more apt to feel it vibrate in his pocket than to hear the ringer.

> Me: Hey, Tully is home. Do you think it's possible to meet me at the greenhouse? She packed a lot, is dead on her feet, and Mom has to head into town.

Mom really does have to go into town for a delivery. I knew that from our talk, plus it's a weekday. After her big events on the weekends, she'll take extra bouquets into town for others to buy. Today happens to be that day.

> Lane: Sure. I've got Dean with me. Do I need more than the two of us?

> Me: No, and hopefully, it won't take too long either. I'm sorry to be taking up so much of your time lately.

Lane would never make me feel like I'm being too much or asking too much. It's one of those habits I'm going to have to work on accepting.

> Lane: Nothing to apologize for. Don't you dare lift one damn thing. You're not ready for my hand on your ass. Yet.

A shiver runs through my body. I have got to

get better *and fast.* I don't want Lane to hold back, ever.

> Me: I can't make any promises ;)

I quit texting. Doing it one-handed hasn't been easy, and there's no way I'll use voice to text in fear of someone randomly making an appearance. I shove my phone into my back pocket, grab my keys, and head back outside. Mom and Tully are long gone.

When Mom is on a mission, she is on a damn mission. Pedal to the metal and ready to get shit done. She's been this way since I was little, never able to sit down and sit still. The television could be on, she'd be sitting in her corner on the couch, and there in her lap, she'd be doing a needlepoint, a word search, or have a puzzle out. Then she's yelling at the game show host on what the answer should be.

It's then that it hits me all at once. I am well and truly my mother. Lord help Lane Johnson. He's going to have his hands full, and not just with my ass.

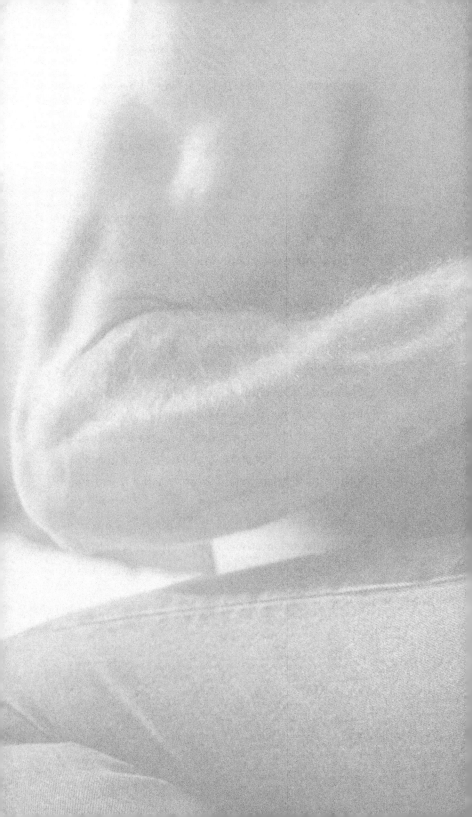

15

LANE

"YOU OVERDID IT TODAY." It's not a question; it's a damn statement. Telling Birdie to sit her ass down and relax in front of her friend wasn't going to happen. I gave her a look, she'd slow down, and when I wasn't looking, she'd go back to unpacking Tully's boxes with her. I grumbled under my breath. My brother Dean would laugh and say something about all women being stubborn.

"Maybe a little, and I know you didn't want me to. Usually, I'd agree with you on this." Birdie is standing too fucking far away from me, and since I can rectify the situation, I do. Rocky is lying in the dog bed I placed near the window in our bedroom. When Dean and I were finished at Tully's, we loaded what was Birdie's and brought it to my place. What I didn't expect to find was not one, not two, but three dog beds for Rocky.

Apparently, he likes to be anywhere his momma is, which means we have a dog bed in our bedroom, the living room, and a spare that she said will probably go in the corner of the kitchen.

"Well, Tully worked her ass to the bone. Stayed back to pick up the pieces of my catastrophe, took care of my boy, picked up her whole life to move here, and did it all with a smile. There was no way I was leaving her to unpack and get settled in alone."

"I get that, but you had me and Dean there. We would have done whatever was needed, babe. I can't protect you when you go rogue. Now you're limping, holding your damn side, and tomorrow, you'll be hurting all over again." I may not be able to heal Birdie overnight, but I can damn sure help relieve some of her aches and pains.

"I have zero plans tomorrow except to have your mom and my mom over. I have ideas for their websites. Plus, with them here, maybe I won't bother you nearly as much." The tips of my fingers pull at the fabric of her tank top, urging her closer to where I've moved. The master bathroom was one of the areas I told my mom to design. She's the reason there's a giant soaker tub. Mom said I'd thank her one day, and that day is going to be today.

"Babe, you're never a bother. You need me, you call me, you text me, you shout my name from the rooftops. I am there." None of this bullshit where Birdie thinks she's a burden. I'll be goddamned if that's ever the case. "You hear me?"

"I hear you, Lane."

"Good. Now, I'm going to get you in the bathtub. You're gonna soak while I make us some dinner, and by no means are you going to unpack those boxes in the living room. I'll put them in the appropriate rooms, and we'll get to them tomorrow when I'm through with work." I lift her shirt up. She knows what I'm about to do, and while only last night and through the night I had no problem taking her, tonight is a completely different story. My cock can wait, and no way am I going to let it do the thinking when she's not feeling her best.

"Stay put. I'm going to start the bath, then I'll help you." I reluctantly move away from her, head to the tub, and turn the faucet on.

"Okay," she replies. The hot water rushes out immediately, and while I know Birdie likes to boil her skin in the hottest water possible, there's no way she can ease herself into the bath. I use my wrist until it's at a happy medium of hot but not too hot. "I only have one problem. I overdid it. I agree with you entirely, but getting in and out of the bathtub might pose a problem. My arms feel like jelly, and my legs do, too." I'm back to her the second I've got the bathwater running and her shirt is barely off her body when she delivers this last set of news.

"Jesus, Birdie, what am I gonna do with you?" I continue undressing her, working the button and zipper of her jean shorts, watching as she does a shimmy until they slide down her legs, lying in a pool of fabric at her ankles.

"Well, I'd say anything you want except for tonight. I wouldn't be able to give myself to you completely. Even I know my limit." I arch my eyebrow up. Birdie does not, in fact, know her limits, or she wouldn't be standing here hurting while I undress her. "Okay, fine. Rain check?" She goes to slip her hand behind her back to unclasp her bra.

"Fucking quit. I'll undress you, help you in the bath, help you out of the bath. Stand there and be still for me, would you?"

"Sir, yes, sir," she jokes. My hand takes over, flicking the clasp in one go. Her tits shake with her laughter, and my eyes leave hers to watch as more of her body is presented to me.

"Birdie, damn it, woman. You are doing nothing in the way of helping my dick stay in my pants." I drop the red lace bra to the floor and watch as her thighs clench together as I breathe in her scent. Fuck, this is going to be a lot more difficult than I planned.

"You act like I can help the fact that my body reacts to the merest touch of yours." I pull the remainder of the lace down her legs. It's a fucking match to her bra, and there she is, soaked. Wetness is coating her bare pussy. I lick my lips, close enough to take from her yet holding myself back in order not to hurt her.

"Same goes, Birdie, same fucking goes. Come on, time to get you in the bath." I'm going to need a minute to calm my shit, or I'm going to strip down and get in with her. My hand clutches hers, and I catch a glimpse of us in the mirror. Birdie is naked to my clothed, she's soft to my hard, she is fucking magnificent, and she's all fucking mine.

"I think I can get in on my own. Getting out will be the hardest," she tells me after a few short steps. We're already in front of the tub, and I shake my head.

"All the same, I'll help you in, just to be on the safe side. Now isn't the time to be independent, baby. Let me help you so you don't suffer." My hand slides from hers to her elbow, holding it in a firm and steady grip.

"One day, you're going to be in a similar position, and just wait and see how you act. You're going to hate every second of me taking care of you as well as not allowing you to do anything." She lifts one leg up, her toes meeting the water first, making sure it's to her liking before placing her foot completely in the water.

"Highly unlikely, but sure, we'll go with that." She grumbles in the back of her throat, and I smile. I'd be the worst patient there is, which is why I plan on not doing anything to turn me into one. I wait until she's completely submerged and the water is up to her shoulders before I turn the water off. "You need anything before I get dinner started?" I ask. Her eyes are closed, head tipped back, and I make a note to get her some shit like a pillow or something, maybe one of those bathtub trays Mom has in hers, and whatever else.

"My phone? I want to check on Tully."

"You got it." I'm bent at the waist, moving a tendril of her hair and placing a kiss on her forehead. I've got to get shit done, and staying here in the bathroom with her won't accomplish cooking dinner, that's for sure.

16

BIRDIE

"I HAVE a major bone to pick with you, Birdie Robertson. Some best friend you are." Lane brought my phone to me along with a pain reliever and a drink to wash it down with—shirtless. The only piece of fabric on his body was a pair of worn-in denim jeans perfectly molded to his thick thighs and firm butt. There's something about Lane barefoot, comfortable in his own skin and looking so damn sexy I have to keep my thighs clenched permanently.

"You can yell at me later. Are you settled? Do you need anything, groceries, a hot meal? And don't you dare say I've done enough, Tallulah Jennings, because I have not done enough." I'm pointing my finger at the wall that holds a mounted television as if she's in front of me. Jesus, Lane really likes his TVs. There's a massive one in the living room, one in the bedroom, and one in the bathroom. He took the bachelorhood meaning and ran with it. I haven't been adventurous enough to check if there's one in the garage or on the back porch. I'd be willing to bet there's one in the garage, at the very least.

"What? No ma'am. Do not even come at me with that line of bullshit. We may not be sisters by blood, but you, my dear, are stuck with me, and we are sisters in every other way imaginable. I'm good on the food. Your mom stopped by with the most delicious thing I've ever put in my mouth." I slap a hand over my mouth, trying not to let the snort loose, as well as the laughter that will come with it. It's impossible. There's no way to hold it in.

"In your mouth? Really? And what have you been putting in it recently?" I ask between short bouts of breathing and chuckling. I have to wrap my arms around my waist to hold myself together. Luckily, my ear and shoulder can hold the phone instead of dropping it in the bathtub.

"I walked right into that, but I wouldn't mind having a taste of Dean. Speaking of, you could give a girl some damn warning." I was pulling up to the greenhouse just as Lane and Dean were. It's not like I could have called to give her a heads-up. She was conked out in the passenger seat, and by the time I got in my own car, they were already there.

"Well, wait till you see the rest of them. They didn't get their nickname, *The Rowdy Johnson*

Brothers, for no reason. They're all easy on the eyes. Mrs. Catherine and Mr. Russell know how to make them. All the brothers have brown hair in different variations, blue eyes, are six foot plus, and goodness gracious, their muscles," I add on the last two for good measure. There's a man standing just outside of the doorway. He doesn't realize I see him, and that works in my favor. I put our call on speakerphone and set it on the ledge of the window. The tub has a view of the snowcapped mountains, green trees, and the cows the Johnsons have grazing top it off.

"I like what I'm hearing. Please tell me more." Tallulah can read the room like no other when we're together. Over the phone, it can be a bit tricky.

"Hmm, let me see. Where do I begin? Oh, I know. The last time I was home, we were all at the rodeo. Each of the brothers competed back then. I'm not sure if they do now. Well, let me tell you, there is something sexy about a man in a cowboy hat, chambray shirt, jeans that mold to their long legs, and a pair of scuffed-up boots. Then you get to see their muscles when they're handling an animal."

Lane chooses that time to barge into the bathroom, the door squeaking on its hinges as he pushes it open, "You looking at me or my brothers, Beatrice Robertson?"

"Gotta go, Tully. My man has entered the chat. I love you!"

"Love you, babe. Enjoy your time. Good night, Lane," Tully says through the speaker, her voice echoing in the bathroom.

"Night, Tallulah," Lane says, looking directly at me as he advances toward me. "Tell me, Birdie, were you looking at my brothers all those years ago, or were you looking at me?" The hot water has done wonders for my ribs. The tightness is easing, and I don't have any problem using my arms to push me upward.

"You, Lane, always you."

"Damn fucking straight, Birdie." He drops to his knees beside the tub, and one hand slides up the inside of my thigh.

"Lane." My head tips back, my eyes start to close, and I spread my thighs for him.

The palm of his hand cups my center in a possessive way. My eyes open, no longer half-lidded. His jaw clenches, his muscles tighten, and I know he's holding back.

"All I see is you, Lane. Please don't stop." I wrap my hand around his wrist, worried he'll take himself away if I so much as wince, and there's no way I can allow that to happen. My hips arch up, silently urging him to keep going, and when I feel the tips of his deft fingers move along my slit, I can no longer hold in the moan. My wetness coats him, my body shivering with the longing to feel him slip inside. On the outside, Lane holds out, strumming my clit with his thumb at one point, and then I feel his finger press against my ass.

"Look at my Birdie, wet and naked for me. You're absolutely aching for me to fuck you with my fingers. I can see it written all over you. Should I give you what you want? Two fingers in your ass, just how you like it, while my thumb fucks your cunt? Yeah, that's exactly what I'm going to do." True to his word, he does exactly what he promises he will. I widen my thighs even farther, feeling the delicious burn of my body stretching to fit his fingers. Lane uses my juices as lubricant to work his fingers, first one, and then two barely pressing in while my pussy sucks greedily at his thumb.

"Oh god." I wiggle myself down on his finger at my ass. I'm filled with want, need, and desire. I'd give anything for it to be his cock instead of his fingers invading me. It's been too many years, too long since I've felt him stretch me. Lane would work my ass with his cock while using his fingers inside my pussy. Each time he pulled out to push back in, his fingers would pick up where his cock left off. "More, Lane."

"We take this nice and slow, or we stop, baby." I'd cry, scream or plead my case if I thought, for one second, it would make him change his mind. Since the likelihood of that happening is slim to none, I do one better. I lift my hips up, meeting him each time he presses in until I've got one finger firmly in place.

"What I wouldn't give to have my mouth on your pretty clit." The visual is absolutely doing it for me. Lane is a giver, not a taker. Even when I try to reciprocate, he feels the need to one-up my orgasm ration to his. There's no changing his mind. He won't stop until I'm completely wrung dry.

"Please, I want that, Lane, so much," I try to persuade him. I drop my hand from where it was on the ledge of the tub, moving it to the nape of his neck to pull his lips closer to mine. If I can't have his mouth on my pussy, I may as well have it in the form of a kiss.

"Next time," Lane promises with his lips while his thumb moves at a faster pace, then one finger is replaced with two. I'm not going to last much longer. The sensation is too overwhelming. Especially when he scissors his fingers inside my ass, stretching me further. "Let go, Birdie, come for me like I know you want to," he breathes between our kisses.

He's dominating my mouth and body. My brain is completely shut off. The only thing I'm thinking about is the pleasure Lane is giving me, and when my body finally computes what he's saying, I let go for him and only him.

Each and every time we're together, I swear it only gets better. Our love grows deeper. We burn hotter for one another, and damn if I'm not loving every moment of it.

17

LANE

"BABE, Rocky has three beds. You want to tell me why he's sleeping in our bed?" Birdie is snuggled into me, her leg hitched over mine, and the boner I've had for more than half the night is not deflating. The show she gave me in the bathtub while I fucked her with my fingers was hot as fuck. The best part about her being in the water was watching her tits bounce up and down, knowing the buoyancy was helping keep her in a relaxed state. It did absolutely nothing for my raging hard-on, but I took care of that in the shower while Birdie watched.

When I got out, she was worked up again. There was no way she would be able to handle much more tonight, so we both got dressed. Her in another one of my shirts and a pair of socks that are so too big, they're slouched around her ankles. She didn't seem to mind. And she makes my clothes look a fuck of a lot better on her than they ever did on me.

"He's always slept with me. Wasn't it you who didn't want to share me? Well, Lane, I think you've met your match. Rocky doesn't like to share either," she breathes into my neck, her nose nuzzling closer to me. I'm pretty sure she'd crawl inside of me if she could.

"One night, and one night only," I grumble. Birdie shakes her head. I can feel the movement, yet I can't see her. I've got my arm wrapped around her body, holding her close to me, and she's on her good side. We'll wind up in a different position throughout the night, but for the most part, when the sun comes up, this is where I find her. "He's lucky he's cute, small, and at the foot of the bed, or I'd be locking him out of the bedroom." Rocky perks up, lifting his head and tilting it to the side. Yeah, the cute multicolored booger will more than likely get his way, just like his owner.

"Okay, Lane." She's placating me while trying not to laugh.

"I guess I better get used to it. One day, it'll be a baby girl or baby boy in bed with us." The tips of her fingers stop their ministrations on my chest. There's no rhyme or reason to the pattern. A soothing sensation for more than her; it helps settle me, and usually, when she stops, the reason is because she's fallen asleep.

"You mean that?" She uses her hand on my

chest to lift up her body. It's a crying shame she's wearing my shirt. I'd much prefer her naked like I am, and I'd have pushed the issue, except there's a nip to the air outside. Birdie knows I run warm. Turning on the heat is a last-ditch effort and only used when the cold really settles in. Now I'm rethinking it. Maybe I should have kicked the heat up in order to have her naked, skin to skin, and should she wake up feeling better tomorrow, well, it'd be a hell of a lot easier access. Sure, Birdie is only wearing a shirt and my socks, but the damn shirt will still be in my way, blocking her tits. There is nothing better in this world than Birdie naked, hair a tangled mess, lips red and swollen from our kisses, and me watching as I fuck my cock into her tight body.

"Fuck yeah, I do. We've got three spare rooms in this house to fill. Two kids to a room, we could carry on the family name and tradition with six little Birdies and Lanes running around."

"Six kids? Are you crazy? They're going to come from my body. My vagina is going to be wrecked. I'll need to do an obscene number of Kegels. Maybe have some kind of surgery to get back to normal. Nope, we're not having six." My hand slides up her back, fingers tangling in the loose chocolate-brown tendrils.

"No other male looks at my woman. You better find a female doctor, Birdie. I don't care if they're getting paid to do what they need to do. No men look at what's mine, ever." She laughs.

This woman thinks I'm joking. I'll be damned. She doesn't realize how serious I am. Juniper can do everything a doctor can do, and at least I know she won't be thinking about my woman in a way I'll have to beat her ass.

"You're being ridiculous, and we're not having six children. You promise me that you won't go over-the-top alpha on whoever my doctor ends up being, and we can compromise on three, with room to talk about a fourth down the road." I'm not really looking for a voice of reason at this juncture of our conversation, yet that's what I'm going to have to take.

"Fine, fine. I'll make sure your doctor is a female anyway," I grouse.

"Thank you, and I'll see what I can work out. I'm not even pregnant. This may take time, so this doctor talk is a little too premature, you know?" There's a playfulness to her tone that's going to get her fucked.

"Shirt off. I don't want anything between us." She sits up, and while the room is dark, the moon is shining through the curtains enough for me to watch as she starts to take off another one of my younger rodeo days shirts. "You need help, or are you okay?" I ask.

"I'm good. The bath helped a lot. The medicine, too. The dinner you cooked was the icing on top." Birdie is talking about an easy dinner I cooked. It didn't take much to put together— hamburger patties, cutting up potatoes to fry up for french fries, and a small salad rounded it out. As far as dessert, the leftover brownies were dwindling down, but somehow, there was ice cream in the freezer. Birdie had no problem heating up the brownies we did have left in the microwave, plopped some ice cream on top, and handed me a bowl before she tucked into her own.

"You gonna get cold?" My hand leaves her hair, sliding around to the front of her body, making sure not to press on her sternum too much.

"Not as long as you're next to me." The palm of my hand cups her breast, my thumb rasping over her pebbled tip.

"You know I'm not going anywhere. Are you going to breastfeed our babies, Birdie?"

"I want to." Her body trembles.

"You gonna let me watch?" I lick my lips, thinking about her nursing our children.

"Of course."

"Good. I'm going to cherish every moment of it. Lie back down before I take this further. I'll be damned if you're too sore to take me in the morning." My cock is rock fucking solid, and I know Birdie is worked up, too.

"Lane." Her voice trembles as she lies back down, this time closer to me than before.

"Not giving us what we both want, even though it's killing me." I nudge her lips with mine, my tongue sliding out until she opens for me. The kiss is filled with need, pent-up desire, and pulling back is damn near impossible. Except Rocky takes that moment to stand up, do a little spin, and then settle back down. "Your dog is a boner killer, baby."

"He is not."

"Birdie, tomorrow night, he's in the dog bed. I'm not going to be taking you in the middle of the night, and Rocky chooses that moment to get excited and interrupt our time." The last thing I want is to be taking Birdie from behind when Rocky gets a wild hair up his ass. Nope, not even going there.

"Fine, he'll go in the dog bed tomorrow night. Love you, Lane, forever," she says quietly.

"Love you, too, Birdie, always."

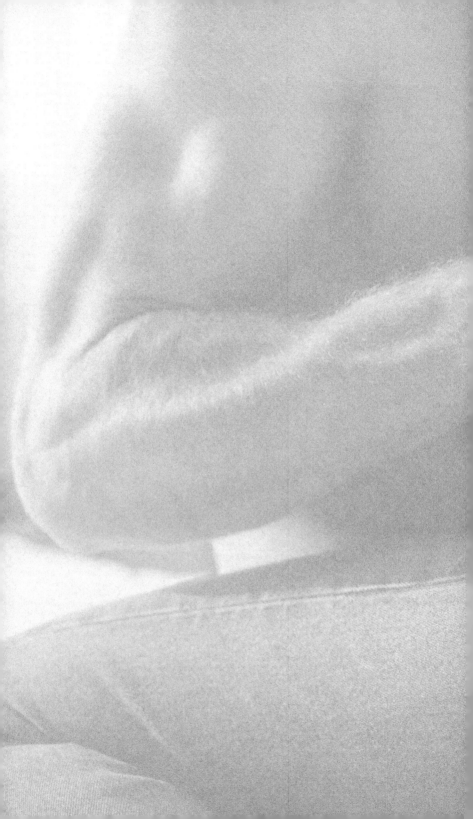

18

BIRDIE

"ROCKY, COME ON, BOY." I clap my hand on my thigh, trying to get his attention. He's fully embracing his life on a ranch. He's also learning to sleep on his dog bed at night, at least when Lane is home. I've yet to tell him Rocky gets on our bed every morning when he leaves to start his day. By the time Lane is back for breakfast, we're out of bed and he is none the wiser. "You're going to get swiped at little, buddy. The barn cats aren't to be messed with. I'd hate to have to take you to see Auntie Tully this early in the morning." My dog has a mind of his own. The little dude is only twenty pounds, but he's full of obstinance and thinks he's Billy Badass.

"Aunt Tully is off the clock, Rocky, so come on." Tallulah opens the back door to Lane's parents' house. She's still settling into her new place and waiting for the moving company to bring our furniture. We had a fully functional apartment with furniture plus accessories, all in good condition. The greenhouse quite literally had the bare essentials, so Tully has been hanging with Mom. Today, I was going to go over to Lane's parents, and she's yet to watch the inner workings of the Johnson ranch. We're going to have lunch, talk shop, and go from there. I already know what my mom is going to say. She wants zero part of technology. Eleanor Robertson feels most at home in her fields of flowers. She likes to joke that she's technologically challenged and, well, I tend to agree with her. Needless to say, she'll tell me to do whatever I want and ask me the price along with the monthly installment to keep it up to date. Easy peasy, lemon squeezy.

The harder part will be the Johnsons' website, making sure the checkout aspect works how they'd like it, and when there's more than one person in on the conversation, it can get tricky. This is why I suggested she and I meet together first, then she could take everything back to the family to discuss how they want to proceed. Their website now has updated prices and the option to contact them via email or contact form. There's also another option to outsource to a call center, where a company can dispatch issues or orders in a timely manner. The price is a bit steeper, and the maintenance is a bit more, as well as making sure that a flood of customers doesn't bog their site down. I can adjust my rate a bit because they are family, after all, but I know the Johnsons; they won't take a handout. Completely understandable. I'm still swallowing my pride due to Lane pushing me in this direction and not getting it on my own.

"Come here, Rocky. Grammy Elie has a treat for you." She walks out with Mrs. Catherine. Tully's shoulders shake with laughter, and I roll my eyes.

"Imagine your mom with grandbabies. They'll be hopped up on sugar the entire time they're with her." Tully knocks into my shoulder. We will both have some free time after the meeting and lunch. So I figure now is as good a time as any to give her the lay of the Johnson land as well as formally introduce all of the brothers.

"Bite your tongue. The two of them would go rabid." I move away from Tully after we give one another a side hug, then approach Mom. She has Rocky eating the treat out of the palm of her hand while she's got him in her arms, and I do the same to her.

"Little traitor." I rub the top of his head.

"Speaking of, where's Case?" I ask Catherine as she comes to stand beside Mom. I immediately give her a hug, and her hand cups my cheek.

"He's napping, but don't worry. The second he hears chitter-chatter and so much as sniffs the air and smells food, he'll be wide awake."

"That sounds entirely like Ryland." When I'd be over here on the rare occasions with Lane, we'd walk in, and Ry would be stuffing his face with the first available thing that was edible.

"You got that right, except Case sleeps through the night, whereas Ryland never did. Now he's getting his payback tenfold. Enough about that. Come in, come in." Mrs. Johnson holds the door open for us. Mom is the leader of the pack with Rocky in her hands, Tully is in the middle, and I'm the caboose.

"Wow, I always wondered how you'd feed and house six men. I can see it now," Tully says as we walk inside the house. The room opens up to the kitchen, and off to the side is a massive dining room table with eight chairs. I know from spending time here that it can seat way more than that. There's also an island almost the length of the kitchen for extra seating.

"It wasn't easy, but we made it through. Drinks are on the counter, the food is ready to eat, and then we'll get down to business," Catherine says just as Case starts squirming through the baby monitor. I watch the screen, ignoring the chatter behind me. Catherine mentioned he'd be up as soon as he heard any type of movement, so now, I'm waiting for my opportunity to have some baby time with Case. When I saw him the other day, my body didn't allow me to do so much as lift my laptop bag. Now, days later, I'm in much better shape.

"Birdie," Catherine calls my name. I look over my shoulder.

HIS TO TAKE   145

"Yes?" She walks toward me, so my gaze returns to the monitor. He's squirming around now, making soft little cooing noises.

"It's killing you to watch and not sneak into his room, isn't it?" she asks.

"So much." I'm wringing my fingers, and I've practically got ants in my pants.

"Go get him, but if he's too heavy to lift while you're recuperating, don't do it. The last thing I need is Lane hollering," she says as I drop my laptop bag to the floor.

"I won't. Promise." Catherine squeezes my hand gently before I head into Case's room, ready to get some baby cuddles.

"SO, are you happy with how things are turning out, business-wise, I mean? It's clear as day Lane will have you knocked up in no time," Tully says as we walk toward the calving area. They've separated the calves from their moms in order to vaccinate and brand them. There are too many times a cow will be found on the side of the road or in a different pasture, especially in these parts.

"It looks like we missed the worst of it," I tell Tully. "And yeah, I mean, the Johnsons still have to go over everything to make sure they're okay with the money side of business. I'm worried I'll be charging them too much, honestly. I mean, Lane and I are a forever kind of deal. Shouldn't I be doing this for free?" This battle has been waging inside of me ever since Lane brought it up. While, yes, it took me a full day to do the Johnsons' and my mom's website, it was more fun than it was work.

"Um, hello? This is me here. I'd do anything for free except refuse a job that was given to me." She waves her hands around in front of us as if there's more news than she's letting on.

"Who gave you a job offer?" The last we spoke, she was still looking at options. The vet in town seems to always be hiring. Though that speaks volumes in itself. Who would want to work at an office with a revolving door?

"No one, promise. My parents offered to give me money to start my own practice, and it rubbed me the wrong way. I told them no, and they said well, how about a loan? Now I'm all jumbled in my head. It would make the best business sense, but it's a lot of money. A lot of what-ifs to think about," my best friend admits.

"For what it's worth, I think a loan would be a great idea. I know there's a lot to think about and numbers to run. It might be worth it in the long run." I knock her shoulder with mine. Rocky is running in front of us, sniffing the air, chasing after birds, only for them to get away and for him to bark in annoyance.

"I'm going to. I like how you avoided the part of our conversation where Lane is going to have you pregnant in a matter of weeks. Imagine him coming inside the house while you were holding his nephew. Shewww, we'd all be a witness to what he'd do to you, and I've only been in his presence a couple of times." I watch as Rocky gets closer to the round pens where the cows are. A couple of the calves' heads are poking through the makeshift fencing. They always think the grass is greener on the other side, and my dog sure likes to test his limits. What Rocky doesn't expect is a cow's tongue coming out to lick him when he's not looking. His little body does a one-eighty, his teeth come out, and so does his bark. The cow jerks back. Rocky keeps getting closer with the yipping, his Rocky Balboa personality coming out when he's not even named after the movie. "Your dog is special, Birdie, real special." Tully and I burst out in laughter.

"I wish my phone was at the ready. Imagine having that pop up in your memories year after year." Our antics draw the attention of the Johnson brothers. Except my eyes are only looking at one. Lane Johnson. Hot, sweaty, and dirty from working all day. This visual is my own personal foreplay, and I'm going to enjoy the show he's giving me when he slowly heads my way. Everyone else disappears.

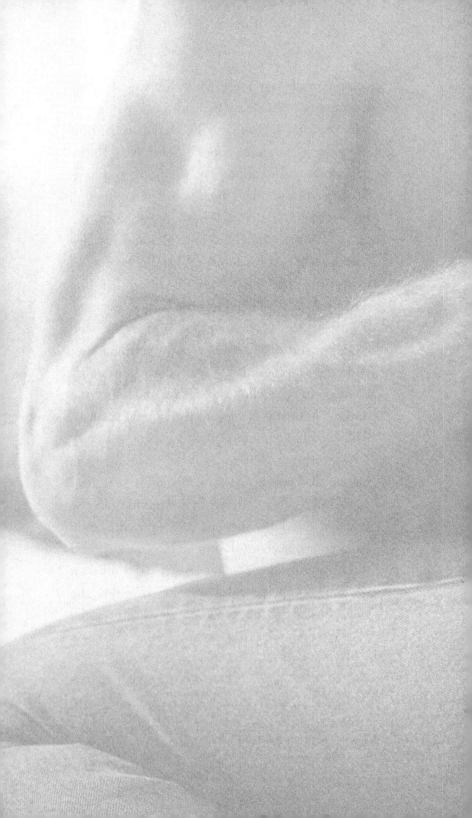

19

LANE

"THIS PLAN IS REALLY GOOD," Lawson states his thoughts. The others are still mulling it over. He's always been the one who can see a number, multiply it, divide it, triple it, and figure out the ins and outs before any of us others could. I smile around a mouthful of the food Mom provides us for lunch when we're working near the house. I was also lucky enough to see my woman, steal a quick kiss, and get inside before Mom started hollering to hurry up.

"I know." I finish my bite, grab my drink, take a quick swallow, and say, "Birdie's the shit. Don't try and finagle the price either. She already gave us a discount. She thought she was being slick, but I got a peek at the paperwork, took a quick look at her website, and saw the starting price. There were other companies that were a lot steeper and didn't have a call center for customer service. Let's just say the price compared to others is a fuck of a lot better."

"Watch your damn mouth," Dad says as I take another bite of food, nodding my head in response. Russell Johnson will listen to us say a lot, but you start dropping F-bombs and more lewd shit, he'll put you in your place.

"I was already going to accept it either way. It was Birdie who was adamant we all take a look first. She didn't want to be underhanded." Mom rolls her eyes in exasperation.

"Speaking of, why does Case smell like Birdie?" Ryland has his son in the crook of his arm while woofing down his own lunch.

"Obviously, Birdie was here. Of course she's going to spend time with Case. You should have seen the way she was with him. It was the cutest damn thing. Makes me want more grandbabies, Lane William Johnson." Mom points at me since I'm the only one in the bunch with a woman. I don't tell her that we're not using anything to stand in the way of preventing a pregnancy.

My phone starts going off in my pocket. The amount of vibrating it's doing means it's a call. I pull it out and see Fletch's name. "Excuse me, I gotta take this call." I push myself out of the barstool and make my way to the door. My family knows enough about the situation. Lawson, more than the others since he and Fletch are close. There was no avoiding the conversation of *Hey, I heard you talked to Fletcher. What's up?* I gave

Lawson a quick rundown, and he told me he'd be there for whatever, no questions asked. Which is why Law gives me a look when I walk by him.

I've got my thumb on the accept button and hit it the minute I reach the back porch. "Hey, Fletch," I answer.

"Hey, Lane, you got a minute?" Well fuck, this must be serious.

"Yep, sure do." I walk toward the barn. We still have a lot of shit left to do in our day, or I'd get in my truck and drive home to Birdie.

"I got the information you were after, pulled some strings. My guy delivered, and you're not going to like this. Fuck, I don't like it either. Kind of wish I were still up there to go after him like I know you will." I keep walking while my stomach sinks to my booted feet.

"Son of a bitch, alright. I'm away from any prying ears. Tell me what you got." My quarter horse, Flash, whinnies when he sees me coming. He probably thinks I've got a treat for him. This morning, I rode him to check along the fence line, and because he thinks he's always got to work along with the others we have here at the ranch, we stalled him for the time being. As soon as the cows are moved to the north pasture, we'll let the horses out to graze.

"Well, Paul Sherman Junior has had several police reports filed against him. Not a single one of them has stuck. Either his victims pull out and go quiet, or they pull a fast one, offer a shit ton of money and sweep it under the rug. I'm willing to bet it's the latter. These people have an in with the higher-ups in the food chain." Flash nuzzles into my chest, begging for attention. My hand brushes his nose, and I scratch while trying to figure out what my next plan of action will be.

"Goddamn it, and with Birdie here in Wyoming, he's thinking she'll just be another victim swept under the rug." I take off my hat, place it on the hook next to Flash's stall, and run my fingers through my hair. I already know what I want to do. I'm ready to hop into my truck, drive to Colorado, and beat the fucking shit out of the little dirtbag cocksucker motherfucker.

"That's about the size of it. I'm going to email you what I can. I know you know this without me saying it, but if something comes up and you're arrested or taken in, my name stays out of it. That being said, I hope you give this piece of shit what he deserves," Fletch tells me.

"You don't have to worry about that. I'll be sure nothing blows back on you. I appreciate it, brother." Flash gets annoyed when I quit rubbing his nose and starts stomping his feet. I swear this boy is an attention whore today.

"Anytime. I'll chat with you later. I gotta get back to work," Fletch says.

"Sounds good." We end the call. There's a lot to unload from the last little bit of conversation, and knowing Fletch, he got me a shit ton of details. Details I'll guard with my life, so Birdie doesn't see them. My woman feels deeply. She'll be full of regret and sorrow if Fletch sends me what I think he will. And there's no damn way I'll let that happen. Birdie has been through enough as it is already. There's no way I'm going to let her keep feeling any sort of pain. Not now and not fucking ever.

"Fletcher get you what you need?" Lawson asks, coming up beside me. The fucker is the tallest of the bunch, has more weight and muscle mass, yet he's still light as a damn feather on his feet.

"Waiting for the email now, but yeah, he did. You wanna take a ride down to Colorado with me?" I already know his answer before he gives it.

"Fuck yeah. You know when you wanna go?"

"Probably the next few days or so. I don't want Birdie to know why I'm heading south. I'm pretty sure there's an auction along the way. Think we can stop on the way back? Birdie doesn't have a horse, and I know she'll be chomping at the bit to get in the saddle soon enough." Two birds, one stone, plus an alibi, all wrapped in one package, neatly tied with a bow.

"Fuck yeah. I'll look at the schedule and make sure it lines up with the auction. The others can handle being on their own for a few days. You clear it with Dad, and all will be well." I pull my hand away from Flash, ignoring his annoyance with me and offering my brother a hand to shake.

"Thanks, man." Law takes my hand. He also pulls me in for a one-armed hug.

"We're family. No need to thank me. Glad you got your girl back, bud." That's that. There's nothing else that needs to be said. Family is love, and love is family, as Grandpa Johnson would say.

20

BIRDIE

"I'VE BECOME the needy girlfriend who misses her man after he's been gone for less than twelve hours, Tully," I tell her. It's been nearly a week of being back home and living with Lane. We've been inseparable since the moment he walked into my mom's house, and now I'm a freaking mess because tonight, I won't have him home to sleep next to. Rocky will snuggle, but he's no substitute for Lane. There's something about falling asleep wrapped in his arms and waking up in them.

"No, you're not. Lane Johnson is sex on a stick. I'd miss him, too," Tully says as she takes a sip of her wine. We're having what we like to call a girls' dinner with a side of wine. When we lived together, it consisted of whatever we could find that required minimal cooking and we'd chow down. Leftovers were among our favorites. Out here in Arrowleaf, there's not a whole lot to choose from where you can get delivery. That's why we're opting for cheese, crackers, sliced meats, fruits, and vegetables.

"That makes me feel marginally better." I'm taking a sip as well, a healthy glug at that. Tonight is going to be a restless night. I can feel it. I'll hear every noise, every creak, and worry tirelessly since he and Lawson are driving without taking any breaks besides food, gas, and the bathroom. On the way down to the auction, the trailer will be empty. It's on the way back that it'll be full. They took a six-horse trailer, which I found odd. The Johnsons' specialty is beef cattle, and the brothers dabble in rodeoing on the side, but for one auction, it seemed excessive.

"Did I tell you I've decided to take the interview at Herbert's Veterinary? I'm going to see what they have to offer. Depending on how it goes, good or bad, I'll go from there." I clap my hands in happiness for my best friend. All week, she's been twiddling her thumbs trying to figure out her next step, and while I don't like the idea of her working for Herbert's, simply because I think she can do a million times better on her own, I am happy for her.

"Hold your horses, lady. Don't go getting excited. I could walk into the office and absolutely hate it." I'm crossing my fingers that she does. It'd be great to get her feet wet, and from what I hear, Herbert's works in big and small animals. I just worry she'll get sucked into a never-ending vortex and come out burned out. Whereas if she'd start up her own, she could do a mobile sort of deal. She'd be able to drive to the ranches around here, which would be a plus. There are a lot of older citizens in the community who love their animals. Getting them to town to see a vet is hard for things like X-rays and whatnot. Plus, she could pick and choose her patients.

"Please tell me you'll take your parents' offer, well, you know." I make the throat-cutting meme across my own.

"Well, about that, I may be able to work here and at the Johnson ranch to build up some money. Plus, your mom said she'd introduce me to a few other farm owners. It'd be routine stuff. This way, I'd have an extra chunk of change and not have to rely on a loan from them completely." Tully has a plan. Now, all she needs to do is execute it.

"I'm proud of us. I know my thing changed your path and our circumstances, and while I'm sorry about putting you in a place where you had to make tough decisions, I am thankful to have a best friend and sister here with me in Wyoming. Is that selfish? Probably. You'll have to deal with me all the same." I've got one hand holding the stem of my glass. The other reaches for Tallulah's hand, squeezing it in solidarity.

"Shut up with that. I didn't want to stay in Colorado anyways, especially not the city. I can understand why you went away to college where we did—the experience, the atmosphere, and the allure. But you and me, Birdie, we're not meant for that kind of lifestyle. Especially not you. Lane, your mom, and Arrowleaf, they're the air you breathe. I hate like hell you had to go through an attack to make you come home, but I'd rather be here than by myself in an empty apartment without my sister from another mister." We both blink back our tears. It's not every day we get emotional, yet when the wine comes out and we're feeling good, the chats go up and down like a roller coaster. I'm only happy that my bruising is finally on the tail end and the twinge of pain is only there every now and then. Come Monday, I'll go see Juni again. Let her take a look, and as long as she thinks I'm okay, I can go about my normal activities. Hopefully, that will make Lane realize that my body isn't made of glass.

"Well, that's bottle number two. You up for another one?" I say after I drink the rest of my wine and reach for the bottle, only to realize it's empty.

"I better not. My interview is tomorrow. Are you staying here tonight or heading back home?"

"Rocky is back at the house. I can't leave him there to his own devices. He'll be sleeping on Lane's pillow, and then I'll really be in trouble." We stand up, pick up our mess, and take it inside.

"You like his brand of trouble," Tallulah says.

"I sure do. Too bad I can't walk home,

though. I've traveled the path between our houses so many times I could do it in my sleep." But after more than a few glasses of wine, driving is out of the question.

"Maybe when the sun isn't close to setting. Plus, your future in-laws are at your mom's, and it's a free ride." Catherine called me earlier today and asked what I was doing. When I told her it was girls' night, she offered to bring me over as well as take me home.

"We'll see about that. I highly doubt it, though. You've seen how protective Lane is. I'm pretty sure he'd put a dang tracking device in my neck if he thought he could get away with it." We finish bringing everything inside. Since we chose to use paper plates, we have less cleanup, so all that's left is the glasses.

"I don't know. I think more like he'd brand you with a tattoo or something. That'd be hot as fuck." Tallulah lets out a yawn, and there's my sign. She'll be passed out in the next twenty minutes.

"It would. Go shower and crawl into bed." I hug her, holding my best friend for a smidge too long for some but not for us.

"Love you. Text me when you're home. I probably won't answer it, but when I roll over in the middle of the night to check my phone, I'll at least see you're safe in Lane's house, tucked into Lane's bed, wearing Lane's clothes."

"Whatever, love you, too, brat." Tully cackles

as I head for the door. I like how close my mom is to my best friend. You can drive, or you can walk. More often than not, the two of them go on foot between the houses. Tallulah doesn't realize how nice it is to know my momma isn't all alone out here in the dead of night. The path between the main house and the greenhouse has solar lights, flowers are planted on either side and with the sun slowly setting, well, let's just say the sky is showing off.

My hands reach out, the tips of my fingers touching the petals of the sunflowers. They're in the early stages of blooming in this section. I'm going to have to come over tomorrow or the next day to make my own bouquet. My website has gotten traction, and with it came a few hours of work, meaning I've been tied to my chair. I should have a day or two free, and I need to spend it with my momma.

"I wish I'd have come with you. It's damn hard to sit my old ass back here while my boys are out there taking care of a small-dicked wannabe of a man." I come around the last bend and see Mr. Johnson. He's got his arm propped up on the bed of the truck, phone to his ear, and he's chewing on a toothpick. "Yeah, yeah, Colorado ain't that far away."

There's no way, none at all. Lane wouldn't lie to me, would he? He wouldn't put himself in jeopardy. That's not who he is. Yet I know that is exactly the man he is. I take a deep breath and

HIS TO TAKE   163

continue to where Mr. Johnson is standing. He's clearly talking to Lane. And I've got a few things to say to him.

"Oh shit, gonna have to call you back," I hear Russell say into the phone.

"Nope, not at all. Can I talk to Lane, please?" It's a question, but my hand is already out, palm up.

"Birdie knows," he says quickly into the phone and then talks to me, "If you think my boy isn't going to make sure the person who hurt you can't hurt you or others, you don't know him as well as I thought you did."

I nod my head. "I'm very much aware of the man you raised. He's a great man, one of a kind. The problem I have with him taking care of the trash is that he didn't tell me first." Russell nods in understanding.

"Birdie, don't be mad at Dad. You want to be pissed, be pissed at me," Lane says before I can get a word out.

"I'm not upset with your father. I'm assuming he was meant to keep me occupied tonight while you go out and play superhero?"

"Not entirely. When I get home, I'll explain everything," he attempts.

"You'll tell me now so I know if I should drive to Colorado and kick your ass, Lane William Johnson." He takes a deep breath as if it pains him to tell me about his operation. Being stupid and attempting a rescue mission, wrapped up in one tiny little present with a big fat bow on top.

"Lawson's friend Fletcher is a cop. He told us what we needed to know, gave us the information we needed, and how to proceed. Does it involve roughing up that dickbag? Sure. It also includes you being safe without having to worry about him ever hurting you again." I should have known Lane wouldn't let this rest. I also should have seen it coming a mile away. He didn't ask if the detective on the case called me back either, which they didn't. I buried my head in the sand and pretended like it never happened. Lane is not the type of man to let things rest when it comes to someone he loves.

"Fine. I'm still kicking your ass when you get home, though. We could have talked about this first." Even as I say the words, my gut and heart are telling me, *Yeah, right, Lane Johnson does things his way when it comes to you.*

"I'm all yours, baby." He's pure golden retriever with a side of Chihuahua when someone hurts his woman or pisses him off. It's kind of hard to be mad at a man with his energy.

"That's the problem, Lane. I want you home, safe, and your arms wrapped around me. Promise me you won't get hurt, or worse, land on his radar and spend time behind bars." My heart beats rapidly at the thought of Lane being arrested. The Shermans are untouchable, it's plain as day when I can't even get a return call or email to see how the investigation is going.

"I don't look good in orange, Birdie. Plus, conjugal visits aren't up there on my to-do list." Lane being Lane, I can't help but laugh.

"You better not. I love you, Lane. Come home safe and sound, please." Russell is standing off to the side with Catherine. She's shaking her head, and I'm sure she's as upset as I am.

"I love you, Birdie. Always. This won't take long. Law and I have this handled. Things go smoothly, I'll be home late tomorrow night. We do have to stop by the auction on the way."

"Alright, I'll text you when I'm home and in bed." There's still a tightness in my chest. This is one of those times I have to let it go and let him do his thing.

"You better, and don't let Rocky in our bed. I already know you've been sneaking him up there when I'm doing morning chores."

"I'm sorry, I can't hear you. You must be going through a dead zone." I make the spit and sputtering noise.

"Yeah, yeah. Night, baby," Lane says.

"Night, Lane." We hang up, and I'm ready to get back to the house, take a hot shower, and settle in for the night. The wine buzz is all but gone, and in its place is worry.

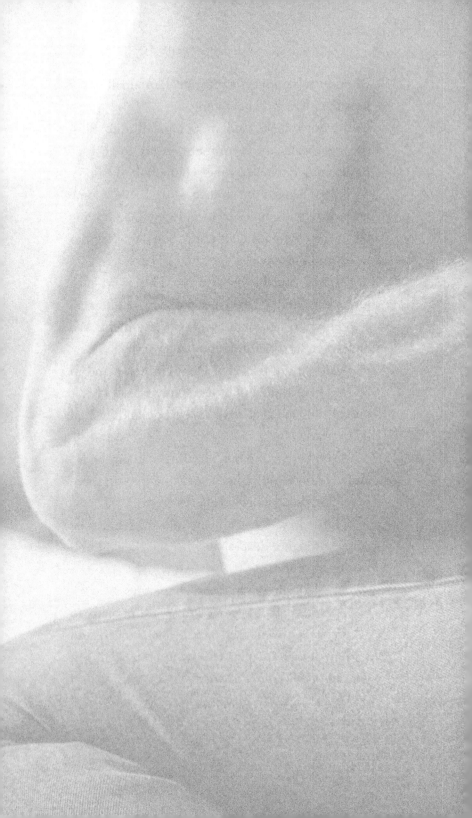

21

LANE

"YOU GOOD?" Lawson asks when I get off the phone with Birdie. The call being on Bluetooth through the truck gave him the whole conversation. We're currently sitting on a side street, waiting for Junior to walk out. Fletch's report gave us every detail about the woman beater. Apparently, he gets off on leaving marks on a woman, threatening them enough to make them do the sort of things no one should ever have to deal with. How this fucker has been able to stay out of the limelight, I've got no idea. I guess that happens when dear old Dad owns a digital social media company and is rubbing elbows with the local politicians. His son must be costing him a fortune in hush money along with a lawyer on retainer for victims to sign a nondisclosure agreement.

"Yep, Birdie may not like what I'm doing, but

168 TORY BAKER

she gets it." At least, I hope she does, with Dad being there and what he told her.

"You better hope, or you'll have a cold bed to go home to," he states, and he probably has plenty of experience in that department since Juniper hasn't given him the time of day.

"She's good." My phone vibrates. I glance at the screen and smirk at the text she sent me.

> Birdie: I love you, Lane. Please
> be safe and come home to me.

"She's real good." My eyes are looking up from my phone as I shoot a quick response back.

> Me: Always, Birdie, I'll love you
> always.

"Ready to rock and roll?" he asks.

"It's go time." I look up from my phone, throw it in the cup holder, and quietly exit the vehicle. Lawson is doing the same. We've got a plan. Doing this at dark is pivotal in getting in and out. Included in the file on Pauly Boy were his usual haunts. It was pure luck that he was coming out of a building with a one-way alley beside us. A little bit of recon showed there weren't any cameras, and now the rest is up to us.

"Hey there, Paul. Wanna have a little chat?" I sidle up to one side, Lawson on the other, and he's already looking like he's going to bolt. I take hold of his arm, squeezing it tighter, and luckily for me, my brother is right in tune with me.

HIS TO TAKE   169

"No, no, I'm good. Thank you, though." We lift him up, and the tips of his shoes drag along the ground.

"Imagine that. He's saying no. Kind of like the women do who he bullies, harasses, beats, and assaults." Fletch did us another solid on how to play this out. Record him but not video. There's some kind of loophole he can handle, and he's going to do that, but with a guy he knows. No one can be trusted in this city.

"They wanted it, I swear." I look at Lawson. He shakes his head in anger. Yeah, I feel the same.

"I'm pretty sure the women you battered did not ask for it. I'm pretty sure no one ever wants to be bruised and used." We walk to the corner. Darkness has settled all around us, and there's only a small light above. Should anyone happen to walk by, all they would see is shadows.

"You have to believe me. What do you want? Money? I've got money. I have loads of it. Don't hurt me," Paul begs. This fucking dick thinks I want money. No amount of cash can replace what he did to Birdie, never mind the rest of his victims.

"Don't want your fucking money." Lawson looks at me. I told him it was going to be me who did the dirty work. I wanted him to be beaten the same way Birdie was, and I'm going to be the one to deliver it.

"What do you want, then?" he asks, dumbfounded. Fucking hell, this piece of shit thinks money can buy him everything. No wonder he is the way he is. Whenever he fucks up, daddy sweeps up the pieces.

"You'll find out soon enough." My fist rears back and goes flying, hitting him right in the nose. Blood spills out. I'm going to have to clean myself up after this.

"Stop, stop, help!" he tries to cry out. Lawson steps into the fold, no longer needing to hold the prick since he's cowering like the little fuckwad he is.

"I want the names of each one of your victims, starting with the most recent." I stand back, letting Lawson get a few licks in. He goes after his stomach, and Paul makes a noise like he's going to throw up. I've had a few tussles with Lawson. It's a wonder Paul is still coherent. He doesn't fuck around; neither do I, for that matter.

"Shit, he's pissed himself," Lawson says. I smirk. This guy is a grade *A* pussy.

"I bet he'll shit himself next," I say.

"I'll tell you. Wait! I'll tell you everything." Barely into this, and he's ready to give it all up. Shit, I wish we had this information. I'd have prevented Birdie from being hurt, then I'd have packed her stuff and brought her home.

"Start talking." Paul is on the ground, curled into a ball, and for each name he gives, my foot finds a place on his body to kick. I'm going to leave him as black and blue as he left Birdie and, with any luck, a fuck of a lot more broken. The rest we'll have to leave up to Fletch. It sucks, but doing this the right way is the only way to do it. That way, he can't hurt another person ever again, and if he does, well, I'll be back to finish the job.

22

BIRDIE

"THANK GOD." I sit up in bed. Rocky jumps off the bed when he hears Lane opening the front door. His little happy yip echoes through the quiet house, and I hear Lane talk to him as he walks down what I'm assuming is the hall, judging by the cadence in his voice. Last night, sleep did not come. I tossed and turned, fluffed the pillows, and moved the covers back and forth. Nothing helped. Not counting sheep, not turning on the television, and scrolling on my phone didn't help either. Instead, I got out of bed, went to the couch, and read until I dozed off, only to be woken up by the sun rising. There was no text or call from Lane, which only made my stomach tighten worse with worry. It wasn't until earlier this evening that he sent me a message saying they were on their way home and my surprise was with him.

"Birdie, you awake?" Lane asks as he walks through the door, the light in the living room glowing behind him. He's stepping out of his boots and pulling his shirt off at the same time. I flip the light on, wanting to see him completely, to make sure he's home in one piece.

"I am now." I tuck my legs beneath me, cross the bed on my knees, and meet Lane at the edge of the bed. In true fashion, I'm only wearing one of his shirts, sans anything beneath. My eyes take him in, starting from the hair on his head down to his face to his now bare chest. His arms are unmarked, and since Lane is unbuttoning his jeans, I'll soon have him completely naked to my gaze. "You're okay?" I ask, taking the fullest and deepest breath since figuring out what he and Lawson had set out to do. The car ride home from my mom's to Lane's, excuse me, *our* house was quiet for a moment after Russell Johnson delivered the news to me and his wife. It was succinct, direct, and no nonsense. What I didn't expect to happen *happened*. Catherine Johnson is not a woman to be messed around with when it comes to her babies. It didn't matter that Lawson was her oldest and Lane was her youngest, varying from thirty-seven to twenty-seven. She grabbed her purse from her lap and repeatedly smacked Russell with it. She was fighting mad, telling him how stupid it was to let them go off after someone like Paul. She was beyond unhappy, and the feeling was and still is entirely mutual. It also sucks to know that everyone knows what happened to me. I get that I'm part of the family, plus Catherine is friends with my mom. Still, it sucked. This is new to me, having a big family. No longer is it only Mom and me. There's Tully, Lane, and with them come all these amazing people who band together, hold you at your weakest, and have no problem fighting your darkest battles.

"I'm okay, Birdie. I'd be a lot better if you lost the tee."

"Is that right? And are we just going to ignore the elephant in the room?" The tips of my fingers find the hem of my shirt and slowly start pulling it up my body.

"Later, much later." Lane replaces my hands as he steps out of his jeans. He's impatient tonight. My shirt is ripped off my body in one fell swoop, and Lane's lips are on mine in a hurry. We're a mess of hands and limbs, both of us needing one another. I'm on my back in a minute, but that's not what I want. I wiggle until I'm on my stomach, getting on my knees and showing Lane how I want him to take me.

"Fuck yeah, you want your ass played with tonight, don't you, Birdie?" His hand squeezes the cheek of my ass, and I widen my stance, arching my back a little bit more.

"Yes, please. God, please." His thumb presses on the tight fissure, applying pressure, and I know he won't fuck me there tonight. That's completely okay. The lube isn't within reaching distance, and neither is my toy, but the fullness of him playing with my back entrance while he takes me with his cock is indescribable.

"Whatever my baby wants." I feel the head of his cock at my entrance, and I push back. I'm tired of waiting. He was gone last night, and yesterday morning is too far away for my liking. "Impatient tonight, are we?" Lane questions, except he's moving his hips, setting a rhythm with me. Every time he pulls out, I push back, his thumb going deeper, giving the perfect fullness when both his dick and finger are inside of me at the same time.

"Stop talking and start fucking," I groan. My hands grip the bedsheets. I'm not going to last, not with the way he's working me up.

"Woman," Lane grunts, his cock pistoning in and out of my wetness. The hand not working my ass slides up my spine. My whole body trembles when Lane's fingers thread through my hair, pull it back, and in doing so, I see stars.

"Yes, Lane. God, yes, right there," I beg for more. Thankfully, Lane knows what I need without me having to describe it. With each slam of his hips, my body gets tighter. My core aches for the release, yet doesn't want the intensity to end.

"Oh yeah, you're there, Birdie. Let go. Fly for me and fucking take me with you." His voice is choppy. Each deep breath he takes is in tune with his thrusting. I close my eyes, tipping my head back farther, and Lane gets the message. He tightens his hold and tugs on the tresses. Stars explode behind my eyes. White static noise tries to cloud Lane saying my name, but I shake my head. I don't want to miss that, ever.

"Birdie," he utters. I lose his thumb in my ass but feel each jet of cum spurt inside me.

"I love you, Lane." I drop to the bed, feeling Lane plaster his body to mine, cocooning me with himself.

"Love you, Birdie, always." He kisses the side of my neck, and damn, I am the luckiest girl in all the world with Lane by my side, forever.

23

BIRDIE

"WELL, don't you look like you're glowing," Tully says as I walk up the bleachers to watch my man. Since I landed back in Arrowleaf, life has been a whirlwind, in a good way. We've seen a lot, gone through a lot, and made it out stronger than ever. Lane and Lawson did most of the legwork, handing off the evidence to Fletch, their friend, who did the Lord's work. Which meant it took time, too much time with the way Lane was grumbling a week later. He and Lawson cornered him in a back alley, beating Paul Sherman Junior like he did many of his other victims. Lane told me how badly he treated other women, not only beating them but beating them into submission to get his rocks off. He was also sexually assaulting women. Yes, women, lots of them, apparently. Some got away, similar to my circumstances. There were others who had it way worse, so much worse, and a few women didn't survive it. So, yeah, while I wasn't thrilled with how they handled it, I accepted it, and now the dust has finally settled. My name and the Johnson name are nowhere near connected to Sherman in any way. We're now free to move on with our lives.

"Who me? Look at yourself. How was your first week at the clinic?" Tallulah didn't hate the interview at Herbert's Veterinary. She said it's a stepping-stone, one to get a rapport with some of the ranchers before she starts her own thing.

"Well, if you consider putting your hand up about fifty heifers to see if they're pregnant or not as fun for an introduction, then it was great." The sarcasm is rolling off her in waves. My nose wrinkles because that's a visual I've seen a handful of times, and I know what comes out of the glove she wears.

"Well, I think I've lost my appetite. Want some?" I offer Tully some of my funnel cake. The drink, she's on her own. I'm entirely too thirsty to even think about sharing my lemon-lime soda.

"Sure. Nothing fazes me after a day at the office." She grabs a big piece of the fried batter saturated in powdered sugar. I do the same before gluing my eyes to the arena.

"I didn't miss anything, did I?" We're sitting at the front of the railing, a place for our feet to rest while also getting an up close and personal view of the Johnson brothers doing their thing. Today, each brother will be in an event. Saddle bronc riding is Lane's area of expertise. The rest of the brothers disperse through other events, such as bareback riding, steer wrestling, tie-down roping, team roping, bull riding, and finally, steer roping. The only thing they don't do is barrel racing, which, hey, maybe Case will do it one day.

"Nope, Lane is up next. And the event after will be Dean." Oh, okay, it seems the attraction between the two may be mutual after all.

"And what event is Dean doing today?" Some of the brothers will switch up, but not Lane. He's always been on a bronc of some kind, saddle or no saddle. The man knows what he likes and sticks with it.

"I think steer roping." Tallulah won't meet my eyes.

"Well then, I guess we better get to watching." The announcer starts talking, shutting me up from finishing any kind of conversation Tully and I were going to have. I hear Lane's number, ninety-nine, his stats and how long he's been riding. My eyes are glued to the chute, trying to get a glimpse of Lane. When I left him, he was cinching his chaps. On the chair was his vest, and then last were his gloves. Everything else, Lawson would help get him ready. The two of them have always been close. The events these past few weeks have made their bond even stronger. I tried to give him a quick kiss before hitting the concession stand, but in true Lane fashion, he had no problem displaying his affection for me. It was toe curling, panty melting, and swoonworthy. Him in his gear, looking like the cowboy he is. Tall, dark, rugged, and he's all mine. And the best part is he has no problem showing everyone in the arena I'm his.

"You can do this, baby." I pick up the necklace around my neck, holding it in my hand, a new adornment Lane surprised me with this morning. The gold heart-shaped pendant is smooth in texture and has a diamond in the center. But on the back, well, that's the showstopper. Lane had our initials engraved as well as *Always*. I swear he has been full of surprises lately. When he came back from Colorado with Lawson, the trailer had a mare and a foal. Maple, a palomino quarter horse with her baby, Willow. I was starstruck, and every spare minute, you can find me with them. Of course, Rocky comes right along with us, and thankfully, I'm healed and not in any pain, so I can ride at a slow trot. Lane's orders, overprotective worrywart that he is.

"He's got this, Birdie." The buzzer rings, it's go time. The chute opens, and the bronc is already bucking, ready to throw Lane off him. My eyes stay locked on him the entire time, making sure his spurs are set above the horse's shoulders until the horse's front feet hit the ground after the first jump out of the chute. His gloved hand is holding on to the thick rein, keeping his body off the horse in order not to be disqualified. I hold my breath, watching as his white cowboy hat flies off on one particular nasty-as-hell buck. My eyes check the countdown in big red numbers. The crowd starts to go wild. Lane has five more seconds, and this horse is giving him a ride that I don't like, but I know will help his numbers in the standings.

"Four, three, two, one," the crowd chants together, and the buzzer goes off.

"He did it, folks! Lane Johnson, coming in with a score of ninety-five point five, taking first place." I'm out of my seat and rushing toward the railing as Lane jumps off the horse. A rodeo clown hands him his white felt cowboy hat. He takes it, saying a quick thank-you without so much as a sideways look. Lane's eyes are on mine, and he's moving quickly. His sole focus is on me, not the crowd cheering, not the arena workers slapping him on the shoulder and congratulating him on an epic ride.

"Lane." I'm laughing and crying at the same time.

"Baby, come 'ere." His hands meet the outside of mine, he's lifting himself up, and I'm getting with the program when one of his leaves the metal bar and goes behind my neck, pulling me to his lips. I dip my head and let Lane have his way with my mouth, much like he does with my entire being. A sigh leaves me, and Lane uses it to gain entrance. He takes over, dominating the kiss. My eyes close, and I enjoy the adrenaline he has pumping through his body, knowing the minute we're alone, Lane is going to have me naked and bent over the nearest available surface. "Fuck, I gotta get back." Lane pulls back, and the crowd is going wild in the distance.

"Okay," I whisper in a daze. Arrowleaf may be small, but we sure do have a lot of townspeople, and the rodeo attracts others from the surrounding areas. I can feel my cheeks flame with heat.

"Always, Birdie, always." He plants another kiss on my lips, hops down, and takes off to the other side of the arena to get out of the way for the next event.

"And that, my friend, is how it's done," Tallulah says when I finally take my seat beside her again. It's then I notice she's eaten the rest of my funnel cake and drank all my drink.

"You're lucky I love you, or I'd make you go stand in the concession stand line," I grumble.

"Please. I'll wait till Lane comes back and tell him you're hungry. He'll do the rest. And I'd be jealous of you if you weren't my best friend."

"If you'd open your eyes, you'd see there's a cowboy with hungry eyes staring right at you," I reply. She shuts her mouth rather quickly and looks up. "Finally, she pays attention." I settle back and enjoy the show. My best friend could potentially become my sister-in-law. Let the matchmaking begin.

EPILOGUE
LANE

Two Weeks Later

"BIRDIE, I think it's time we talk." I walk through the house after a day of mending fences. I swear to fuck, if that big mean bull doesn't quit trampling the barbed wire to get to the heifers next door, I'm going to take him to the auction myself. It seems like once a freaking month, I have to fix his fuckup, and then we have to call Herbert's, who sends out Tully to clean up the wounds we can't. We could bypass the whole process and put the money in Tallulah's back pocket, except she's one headstrong woman.

"What do you mean we need to talk? Is something wrong with the family?" she asks, standing at the stove making dinner.

"No."

"Rocky?" Lately, he's been glued to my side when I leave after doing my morning work.

"Nope."

"Maple or Willow?"

"Everyone is fine. It's you we need to talk about." Her eyebrows shoot up, and she stops kneading the dough she was working on. Eleanor gave Birdie some sourdough starter, and she's been on a kick ever since. There's a fresh loaf waiting when we're down to the last few slices, and I'm not complaining a bit. Birdie in the kitchen, Birdie with the animals, Birdie working, and Birdie when I've got her naked in any way will always be my favorite.

"What do you mean?" She drops the dough into the loaf pan to rest, throws a towel on top of it, and then moves to the sink.

"Baby, you've been home for how long now? We haven't used protection, and you've not had a period. It's time to take a test." After work, I went into town. I didn't want to drive to the nearest grocery store, which is damn near thirty minutes away. The next closest place is one of those damn dollar stores. It's as good as any other place, even though they jack the price up for convenience. This couldn't wait.

"Um, Lane, how do you know so much about my body?" Birdie washes and dries her hands. I walk closer, the bag swinging in my fingers, and Rocky climbs out of his bed, stretching like he's

HIS TO TAKE   189

worked all day. I dropped him off before heading to the store. Birdie wasn't in the kitchen, so she probably didn't even notice. Once she's in the zone, she's in the zone, especially with work or in the kitchen. She tunes everything out or wears headphones to tune the background noise out. I didn't understand the need at first until she explained that in college, there wasn't a choice. Dorm life wasn't about studying for her room-mate. Partying was. The library wasn't much better either, so now it's something she does auto-matically. Tallulah does the same thing appar-ently, except hers is to listen to romance novels. Both the girls have a wine night once a week and talk about their latest read. That'll be coming to an end if my suspicions are right, the wine aspect at least.

"Babe, my dick has been in you nonstop. Besides the one night Law and I went down to Colorado. You think any kinda man wouldn't put two and two together?" I drop the bag on the counter. The three boxes of pregnancy tests tumble out. There were a lot to choose from, one claiming to be an early response, another claiming to have the fastest response time, and then another cheaper one.

"I think you may have gone overboard, Lane," she says, eying the counter. A tentative hand reaches for the early response box, and I think the idea is finally settling in.

"Maybe, maybe not. Figure they don't expire,

so they'll eventually get used." I watch as her unoccupied hand trembles as it goes to her mouth, and that's enough of that. "Take the test, Birdie. I'm here, always. I'm never letting you go again. You set out to achieve your goals. Now it's time we accomplish the ones we want to achieve together." I round the corner. My hands cup her cheeks, and she moves her hand away from her mouth to hold my wrists.

"What if it says I'm not pregnant, though?"

"Then we keep trying until you are." I press my lips softly to hers for a moment, knowing this could easily change into a naked kind of moment. "You good?" She takes a deep breath.

"I am. We're really doing this, aren't we?"

"Yeah, Birdie, we are." I take the decision out of her control, grabbing the box from her hand while the other laces our fingers together. I'm all but dragging her to the nearest bathroom, which so happens to be the half bath off the living room. A two-story ranch house with the master bedroom downstairs is going to come in handy after the news we receive today.

"No way, you are not. Lane William Johnson, I will kick you in the balls, and then children won't be a problem." I shake my head. I've seen Birdie in every way imaginable. This isn't something I feel the need to be away from.

"Babe, you think I'm worried about you peeing in front of me? One day, I'm going to be holding your hand while you deliver our baby.

This is nothing." Birdie crosses her arms over her chest. My eyes zero in on her tits and I lick my lips, knowing we'll be celebrating in the next ten minutes. She's going to be riding my face, and my hands are going to be working her nipples.

"That's well and fine when it happens, but this is a hard no, Lane."

"Leave the door open, and I'll stay out here with my back turned," I compromise.

"Fine. Insufferable, always-gets-his-way man." She mutters that last part, but I'm already doing what I said I would. I use the wall to prop myself up. Birdie rips open the box as she continues talking in a hushed tone. From what I can surmise, it's the directions. Finally, after what seems like fucking forever, I hear the zipper of her jean shorts followed by her taking care of business. My head tips back, and I close my eyes. It's time I made Birdie mine permanently. The ring I've had forever is going on her finger tonight, regardless of the answer we receive. I'm tired of her not having my last name or a ring on her finger. I've already got the gold-and-diamond band in my possession. It's soft, delicate, and nothing overly flashy. One thing about Birdie is she's not much for showing off. Hell, it's why she's had the same vehicle for years.

"Alright, you can come in now." A turn of a corner and three steps, then I'm there with her. She's washing her hands, and her eyes stay on the test the entire time.

"You good, baby?" I come up behind her, my arms wrapping around her middle, chin settling on her shoulder. Birdie's eyes meet mine in the mirror for a moment and then slide back to the test.

"I am. Do you see what I see?" I look at the test and see a positive sign.

"Fuck yeah, Birdie. You're going to have my baby, you're going to be my wife, and I'm going to love you, *always*."

I hope you enjoyed Lane and Birdie's story and will consider leaving a review. If you'd like a bonus scene of His to Take click the link below for more!

His to Take Bonus Scene

Coming next is His to Please, Dean and Tallulah are up next in book 2 of The Rowdy Johnson Brothers and theire story releases Feb 18th!

Amazon

Prologue
Dean

TWO WEEKS *Earlier*

"You have to be quiet Tully, anyone could walk in on us at any time," Tallulah, my future sister-in-law's best friend is in the tack room with me. She's bent at the waist, pants at her ankles, and I'm working my cock in and out of her pussy, "Fuck, I can feel how much you like that idea." I grunt with each thrust of my hips. The idea of Tallulah getting caught is hot as fuck, she may not say it with words, but her body is telling me exactly what she wants. Her cunt tightens, she only gets wetter, and damn this condom for dulling the sensation. I'd take her raw if she hadn't made it clear that there will be no little Dean or Tully's running around the ranch. Apparently, she isn't on birth control and I'm fine with that, for now. Until Tully gets it through her stubborn ass head that she doesn't have to do it all on her own in the way of working with large animals in the veterinarian field. Tallulah could have paved her own way without having to deal with Herbert and his simple-minded bullshit.

"Dean," she says my name in a soft throaty purr. My hands slide beneath her body, moving upwards until my hands cup her tits. she pushes back into me, head tossing back, hair cascading over her naked back. Tallulah likes the idea of getting caught, and it's only makes her wetter, I grunt into her ear with each thrust of my hips. Tallulah is bound and determined to keep us fucking like rabbits quietly.

"Fuck Tully," I almost stop moving, the way her pussy clenches on my dick has me ready to come and I'll be damned if I'm ready for that to happen yet. We're only getting started.

"Don't you dare," I'm pulling her body up, her back is to my front, and while I' might have slowed my pace. I damn sure didn't stop.

"Not a fucking chance, Tully, not fucking ever," the need to be deeper, to feel every ripple, every pulse, and the way she gives over to her pleasure. It's an incredible sight to see and to know I'm the one that Tully falls apart for, fuck that's something else entirely. "Mouth, sunshine. I need your mouth," a few more skillful movements and I know Tallulah enough that she'll be coming in a matter of moments. The only way to keep her quiet is to swallow her moans. One day soon, very fucking soon we won't have to hide what we're doing. And it's not because of my brothers or her best friend. It's all on Tully, she won't accept help and won't listen to reason. And I get it, partially doesn't mean I have to fucking like it. Not one single bit. Birdie, Birdie's mom, my mom, and even Lane tried to talk to her. She refuses to take handouts, at least right now. I also know a bit of information about old man Herbert, his son left town and didn't look back, started working for himself. There's other shit going down with Herbert Veterinarian Clinic, things that I'm not telling Tallulah in case nothing comes of it.

"Dean, more honey, please," she sighs as my mouth slants over hers, my tongue presses in, seeking entrance, and she doesn't resist. My hand moves away from Tully's breasts, a fucking travesty but what's to come will only make her impending orgasm that much stronger. While I dominate her mouth and body, my hand slides to her throat, fingers wrapping around her throat. My thumb on her pulse point, pressing into it, and with my mouth on hers. I keep thrusting my cock in and out of her tight heat and Tully falls apart. She pulls me right along with her, I have a hard time keep my mouth sealed to hers, the way Tully has me wrapped up in knots, only getting small doses of her. It's not fucking enough, it won't ever be, and this damn keeping things quiet has to stop.

"Dean," her eyes are closed and she nuzzles into the side of my neck, I can each inhale and exhale from Tully trying to catch her breath. It's nice to know I'm not the only one unaffected.

"Tallulah," I hold her body to mine, tightly as we come down from our combined orgasms. Sucks I won't be able to stay inside her wet depths much longer, I've got to deal with the condom, clean her up, and then both of us need to get dressed. We've probably been in here long enough. She came to look after our prized bull. Lately he's been having issues mounting the heifers, we called Herbert's since Tallulah made it clear we were to do things by the books. I get that she has an end game, start a rapport with the ranchers before going out on her own. It's a plan, probably smarter than us giving her the leg up we can, but watching her dead on her feet every day, working weekends, and doing the grunt work only because she's new in town is fucking bullshit.

"Have you seen Tully?"

"Fuck," I whisper, her body arches away from me, causing me to lose her heat. I'm left standing with my jeans around my ankles, my cock in the wind, and Tallulah is scrambling to get pick up her clothes.

"I'm screw, oh my God. I'm so screwed, my job is going to be taken from me and I'm going to be known as the town harlot," Tully is attempting to shove her pants on without her lace thong, jumping up and down. I'm attempting not to laugh, who the fuck says harlot in this day and age.

"Sunshine, breathe," I pull my jeans up, I'll have to deal with the condom in a minute, "They've already left, you've got a few minutes to pull yourself together, and not one fucking person in this town would think that of you," I'd make damn sure of it too. I bend down to grab the remainder of her clothes, pocketing her thong. She's already got her jeans on, no use in her getting undress to redress.

"You don't know that. I'm an outsider. It's bad enough the employees at the clinic hate me. Them finding out would only make it worse," Tully admits and this time it's my body locking up, irritation is thrumming in my blood stream.

"They giving you hell besides the usual?" I ask, she puts on her bra, then her shirt. I've lost every semblance of her naked body and it's a damn shame.

"It's nothing, forget I mentioned it," Tully says stepping in her boots, smoothing down her shirt then taking her hair out of a lopsided pony-tail before redoing it.

"Tully, all you gotta say is the word," she goes to walk around me and I stop her.

"I'm fine Dean, promise. I've got to get back to work, I'll see you later," Tallulah is anything but, every man worth his grain of salt knows that when I woman says she's fine. She goes to the tips of her toes, pressing her lips to mine, shutting me up. Tallulah may think she's got to do everything on her own, she's about to learn that I'm not letting my woman at it alone.

Amazon

ABOUT THE AUTHOR

Tory Baker is a mom of two teenagers and a dog mom to one wild and active Weimaraner, Remi. She lives in a small coastal town on the east coast of sunny Florida. Oftentimes you'll find her outside soaking up the rays with at least three drinks surrounding her, a wandering imagination, and a notebook in hand where she's jotting down a plot for her next story. She's a lover of writing happily ever afters with Alpha heroes and sassy heroines.

Sign up to receive her **Newsletter** for all the latest news!

Tory Baker's Bombshells is where you see and hear all of the news first!

ALSO BY TORY BAKER

Men in Charge

Make Her Mine

Staking His Claim

Secret Obsession

Baring it All

His for the Taking

Needing His Touch

Billionaire Playboys

Playing Dirty

Playing with Fire

Playing With Her

Playing His Games

Playing to Win

Vegas After Dark Series

All Night Long

Late Night Caller

One More Night

About Last Night

One Night Stand

Hart of Stone Family

Tease Me

Hold Me

Kiss Me

Please Me

Touch Me

Feel Me

Diamondback MC Second Gen.

Obsessive

Seductive

Addictive

Protective

Deceptive

Diamondback MC

Dirty

Wild

Bare

Wet

Filthy

Sinful

Wicked

Thick

Bad Boys of Texas

Harder

Bigger

Deeper

Hotter

Faster

Hot Shot Series

Fox

Cruz

Jax

Saint

Getting Dirty Series

Serviced (Book 1)

Primed (Book 2)

Licked (Book 3)

Hammered (Book 4)

Nighthawk Security

Never Letting Go (Easton and Cam's story)

Claiming Her (Book 1)

Craving More (Book 2)

Sticky Situations (Travis and Raelynn's story)

Needing Him (Book 3)

Only His (Book 4)

Carter Brothers Series

Just One Kiss

Just One Touch

Just One Promise

Finding Love Series

A Love Like Ours

A Love To Cherish

A Love That Lasts

Stand Alone Titles

Nailed

Going All In

What He Wants

Accidental Daddy

Love Me Forever

Gettin' Lucky

It's Her Love

Meant To Be

Breaking His Rules

Can't Walk Away

Carried Away

In Love With My Best Friend

Must Be Love

Sweet As Candy

Falling For Her

All Yours

Sweet Nothings Book 3—Tory Baker

Loving The Mountain Man

Crazy For You

Trick— The Kelly Brothers

Friend Zoned

His Snow Angel

223 True Love Ln.

Hard Ride

Slow Grind

1102 Sugar Rd.

The Christmas Virgin

Taking Control

Unwrapping His Present

Tempting the Judge

Naughty Noelle

ACKNOWLEDGMENTS

This is about to get very long and very wordy because that's just who I am. I've got so many people to thank and shout out that I hope no one is forgotten. When I set out about change this year, I was all freaking in. I'm extremely fortunate you all are taking this wild ride with me. The depth in these stories it fills my heart up with a joy I lost along the way and my cup couldn't runneth over without your support!

To my kids: A & A without you I'd be a shell of myself. You helped me find myself in a moment of darkness. Thank you for picking up the slack around the house while I was knee deep in this deadline, cooking, cleaning, and taking care of Remi (our big lug of a Weimaraner). I love you to infinity times infinity.

NaShara McClaeb: Ya'll can thank her for that gym scene in Staking His Claim. She still sends me so much inspiration, tells me when my sentences ar run-ons or incomplete. Gives me so much shit about y'all vs ya'll. It's ya'll for this girl by the way. There have been many a conversations we've had about a story. Every time I struggled, she was there to kick my ass into gear. I can't thank you enough! Also, she's my sports partner through and through

Katie Cadwallader (Okay Kyle it's Welter but iykyk): This woman right here is responsible for so freaking much and not just my amazing cover photos. We bounce off each other for ideas, she's the only person I know who is so creative and still have the mindset of a business consultant. Her family has become an extension of mine and I can't wait to see her again!

Jordan: Oh my lanta, the hand holding, the me calling you hysterically crying or laughing, day or night, good or bad. I love you bigger than outer space. If it weren't for you pushing me to write, to see the potential in me, I wouldn't be here.

Mayra: My sprinting partner extraordinaire. Girlfriend, we made it through 2022 ahead of schedule. One day I will fly my butt to California to hug you!

Julia: How do you deal with me and my extra sprinkling of commas? The real MVP, the one who deals with my scatterbrained self, missing deadlines, rescheduling like crazy, and the person I live vicariously through social media.

Amie Vermaas Jones: Thank you for always and I do mean always helping me on my last minute shit. It never fails that I'm sending you an SOS asking for your eyes. Beach days are happening and SOON!

Thank you for being here, reading, not just my books but any Author's stories. We do appreciate you more than you know, the reason why we can live out our dream is for readers, bloggers, bookstagrammers, bookmakers, Authors, and everyone in between. THANK YOU!

All this to say, I am and will always be forever grateful, love you all!

Printed in Great Britain
by Amazon